Without

A Doubt

ROBIN JONES GUNN

PUBLISHING

COLORADO SPRINGS, COLORADO

WITHOUT A DOUBT

Copyright © 1997 by Robin Jones Gunn
All rights reserved. International copyright secured.

Library of Congress Cataloging-in-Publication Data
Gunn, Robin Jones, 1955–
    Without a doubt / Robin Jones Gunn.
        p.   cm. — (The Sierra Jensen series ; 5)
    Summary: Although she is excited about the prospects of a great summer when
both Randy and Drake show an interest in her, 16-year-old Sierra finds that her inex-
perience with dating leads to confused, unsettled feelings.
    ISBN 1-56179-519-4
    [1. Christian life—Fiction. 2. Interpersonal relations—Fiction. 3. Brothers and
sisters—Fiction.] I. Title. II. Series: Gunn, Robin Jones, 1955– .   Sierra Jensen
series ; 5
PZ7.G972Wi   1997
[Fic]—dc20   96-38991
                                            CIP
                                           AC

Published by Focus on the Family Publishing, Colorado Springs, CO 80995.

Distributed in the U.S.A. and Canada by Word Books, Dallas, Texas.

Scripture quotations taken from the *American Standard Bible*, ©1960, 1963, 1968,
1971, 1973, 1975, 1977 by The Lockman Foundation. Used by permission.

The C. S. Lewis quotation on page 119 is taken from C. S. Lewis, *The World's Last
Night and Other Essays* (San Diego: Harcourt, Brace and Jovanivich, 1973).

Focus on the Family books are available at special quantity discounts when purchased
in bulk by corporations, organizations, churches, or groups. Special imprints,
messages, and excerpts can be produced to meet your needs. For more information,
contact: Sales Dept., Focus on the Family Publishing, 8605 Explorer Dr., Colorado
Springs, CO 80920; or phone (719) 531-3400.

This is a work of fiction, and any resemblance between the characters in this book and
real persons is coincidental.

Editor: Janet Kobobel Grant
Cover Illustration: George Angelini
Cover Design: Praco, Ltd.

Printed in the United States of America
97 98 99 00 01 02 03/10 9 8 7 6 5 4 3 2 1

For our son, Ross

As you enter high school,
may you have lots of buddies,
and may you all draw each other
closer to the Lord

Chapter 1

SIERRA JENSEN TUGGED ON HER BASEBALL CAP'S brim and wiggled her fingers to tighten her grip on the bat. Her long blond hair poked through the back of the cap in a wild, curly ponytail.

"Hey batter, batter, batter, swing!"

Shooting a glance toward her friend Amy Degrassi, the heckler in the outfield, Sierra lowered her chin and eyed the pitcher.

"Come on, Dad," she called out. "Give me all you've got. I can hit anything you can send over this plate."

Sierra could tell her dad was enjoying this perfect, sunny Oregon Sunday. It was Father's Day, and he was surrounded by his family and a dozen neighbors and friends. Mount Tabor Park brimmed with families firing up barbecues, tossing Frisbees, and pushing toddlers on the swings. Only the Jensen group, with enough players to form two teams, occupied the baseball diamond.

"Come on, Lovey!" Sierra's Granna Mae called from her folding lawn chair planted behind the backstop. "Show me what you're made of!"

"I'll show you what I'm made of," Sierra muttered, adjusting her position. "I'm made of steel."

All eyes were on her. Mr. Jensen let loose with a slow-pitched, underhanded curve ball. Sierra swung and missed.

"Stee-rike one!" Randy Jenkins yelled, rising from his crouched catcher's position behind Sierra.

"You don't have to tell the whole world," Sierra snapped playfully at him.

Randy tossed the softball back to Sierra's dad and wiped his glistening brow. He wore his baseball cap backward and sported his familiar crooked grin.

"That's my job, Missy. That's why they pay me the big bucks."

Sierra liked the way Randy could handle her teasing and dish it right back. Ever since they had attended a concert together a few weeks ago, Randy had come over or called her every day. She loved the attention.

His family had joined hers for this picnic celebration, and Randy's dad hollered from his spot on third base, "Let's go, Sierra! Bring me home, Slugger!"

With a glance at the player on third, Howard Jensen pitched the ball right over the plate. Again Sierra swung too late.

"Hey, I wasn't ready!" she squawked. "That shouldn't count."

"Stee-rike two!" Randy bellowed.

Sierra shot him a fierce look and choked up on the bat. With a slight sway, she watched her dad catch the ball, grind it into his mitt, and wind up.

"Hey batter, batter, batter, swing!" Amy chanted from the outfield.

"Hit a homer, Lovey!" Granna Mae called.

"Right here. That's it," Randy muttered. "Send that baby right into my mitt, Mr. J."

Sierra ignored them all. She didn't blink as the ball came toward her. In perfect motion, she swung. The bat connected with the softball, and a beautiful SMACK sound filled her ears. Dropping the bat, she took off running for first base, not daring to look where the ball was flying. Tagging first base, she charged on to second with a quick glance at home plate, where Mr. Jenkins had arrived safely and was now cheering her on to victory. A quick tap at second, and her feet flew toward third base.

"Come on home, Sierra! You've got it! Come on!" Randy's dad yelled, waving his arms. Randy stood in front of him, one foot on home base, mitt in place, eyes fixed on the outfield.

Visions of glory danced in her head as Sierra gulped a quick breath and pushed herself off third base. She loved this adrenaline rush. If she made it home, their team would win, and she could thoroughly harass her eldest brother, Wesley, who had predicted that his team would win, especially since their dad was on the pitcher's mound.

Sierra pushed her leg muscles forward, her heart pounding. Only a few more feet. She felt her baseball cap coming off as she charged to her goal. Randy positioned himself like a brick wall beside home base. His arms reached up into the air.

She blasted toward him, screaming, "Move!"

With a final spurt, Sierra slid toward the base just as Randy jumped, reaching with his mitt. Her left leg skidded in the dirt, and her right foot caught Randy's, pulling him down with her in a tangled heap.

A cloud of dust surrounded them as Randy's dad yelled, "Safe! I saw it. She was safe!"

Coughing and shaking her now capless curls away from her face, Sierra tried to move. Randy regained his balance first and stood. He offered her a hand up. Sierra brushed herself off and coughed again, looking at her opponent. Dirt clung to his thick eyebrows like drops of rain on a screen.

"You're out," he said in a low, unemotional voice.

"What do you mean I'm out?" Sierra shouted. "I'm safe, and you know it!"

Randy grinned and smugly held his catcher's mitt in front of her. He opened it slowly and dramatically, his eyes glued on Sierra's face as he prepared to show her the evidence. What Randy didn't see was the way the ball fell out just as he opened the mitt.

"Ha!" Sierra said, pointing. "I'm safe! You have to actually *catch* the ball before you can get someone out in this game, and it appears you have an empty mitt, buddy."

Randy looked at the mitt, looked at Sierra, and then gazed down at the ball in the dirt.

"I had it," he protested.

"Doesn't matter," Sierra said. "You have to keep it if it's going to count."

The other players had joined them at home base, each one barking out opinions.

"I'm safe. We won. Deal with it, Jenkins!" Sierra teased. As she started to stand up, a slice of pain seared her left leg. Rivulets of blood coursed from a long scrape that began above her knee and ran all the way down her leg.

Amy, arriving from center field, noticed it, too. She had Sierra's runaway baseball cap in her hand and said, "That is so gross. How could you slide on your bare legs like that? You'd better clean that out, Sierra."

"We won!" Sierra answered Amy triumphantly. "I told you we would win."

"It was rigged," Sierra's brother Wesley said. He had the bat in one hand and a mitt in the other. Of all the Jensen kids, Wes most resembled their father, with his straight nose, wavy brown hair, and slim build. He especially looked like their dad around the eyes. When he smiled, he had the same pattern of laugh lines stretching like party streamers from the corners of his eyes. Only their father's were deeper and longer.

"Guess your star pitcher was no match for me," Sierra teased her brother.

"You were out, and you know it," Wes said, snatching Sierra's baseball cap from Amy's hand and plopping it backward on Sierra's head.

Sierra's six-year-old brother Gavin had joined the

mob. When he saw Sierra with her cap on like Randy's, he said, "Now you and Randy are twinners!"

To her surprise, Randy slipped his arm around her shoulder, pulled her close, and repeated, "That's us. Twinners."

Sierra heard a camera click and looked beyond Gavin and Wesley to see her brother Cody and his wife, Katrina, who had just arrived with their toddler son, Tyler.

"That'll be one for the scrapbook," Katrina said with a wink at Sierra.

The sharp pain in Sierra's leg had suddenly become intense. Wiggling out of Randy's one-armed hug, she said, "I'll be back," and with a slight hobble, she headed toward the rest room.

She heard Amy behind her saying, "Do you want me to bring over a Coke for you, Wes? I was going to get one for myself anyway."

The thought had crossed Sierra's mind more than once that Amy might have a crush on Wesley. Now she was sure of it. Serving men food seemed to be Amy's way of reaching their hearts. It didn't seem to matter to Amy that nearly five years stretched between her age and Wes's. Until a week and a half ago, all Amy could talk about was Drake, a guy from school. That was until Wes moved home for the summer from Corvallis, where he attended college. Now Amy was over all the time, and her dark Italian eyes followed Wes wherever he went.

Sierra didn't know how she felt about Amy flirting with her oldest brother. She couldn't blame Amy for being attracted to him. Besides his good looks, Wes was patient and kind, and he loved dogs, just like Amy did. Two nights ago, Wes had taken their bumbling St. Bernard, Brutus, for a walk, and Amy had volunteered to go with him. Sierra went along, feeling like a chaperone. Wes had been nice to Amy and talked to her about the things she was interested in. That's the way he was. Sierra doubted if Amy understood that.

Inside the chilly park rest room, Sierra picked at the wedged brown paper towels in the steel holder until she freed a corner. The first one she pulled came out in shreds. The next towel cooperated. She wet it and began to clean the stinging scrape on her leg.

She certainly understood Amy's attraction to an older guy. Sierra had been interested in an older guy named Paul, who had pretty much ruled her dream life for the last five months. Then Paul left for Scotland, and that was the end of that fantasy. Ever since Paul left, Randy had been, well . . . attentive. And she liked it.

The blood cleaned up quickly enough, revealing a small cut. It had stopped bleeding, but the cool water felt good as she held the paper towel to her leg.

So here she was. The summer stretched out before her, and her calendar was full of plans with her friends. The best part was, for the first time in her life, Sierra had a bedroom all to herself. Two days earlier, her only sister, Tawni, had taken off for Southern California, where she had big plans to break into modeling. Tawni had invited Sierra to make the two-day drive with her, but Sierra couldn't arrange the time off from work. She had already asked Mrs. Kraus at Mama Bear's Bakery for time off to go on a backpacking trip with her youth group at church. And then she had asked for a week off in August to travel to California for the wedding of her friends Doug and Tracy.

Tawni had understood. Their good-bye had been a tearful one, and Sierra wondered if she had made the right choice—backpacking with Randy and Amy over going with Tawni. Surprisingly enough, after 16 years of living side by side as feuding sisters, she and Tawni were suddenly becoming friends.

Friends. Sierra liked that word. She had good friends, and she was looking forward to the fun they were going to have together this summer. Only one nagging question kept running around in the back of her mind. But she was ignoring it. For weeks she had been ignoring it.

After splashing some cool water on her face and neck, Sierra felt better. She turned her cap around, pulled her ponytail through the hole in the cap, and was ready to join the others. She stepped outside the dark, musty bathroom and into the bright afternoon sun.

Randy stood a few yards away, leaning against a tree. Obviously, he had been waiting for her. Randy smiled and walked toward her. The nagging question surfaced again: *Do I know what I'm doing?*

Again Sierra brushed the question away. Greeting Randy with a smile, she said, "No stitches required."

"That's good," Randy said. He looked almost shy as he

stepped forward and held out his hand.

Not sure what else to do, Sierra slipped her slightly damp hand into his, and they walked together across the lush grass toward the picnic tables where the others were now gathered. A summer breeze laced its way through the ancient cedars towering above them. It seemed to Sierra as if the trees were whispering to each other, "Look! Look! They're holding hands. Isn't that cute? Oh, he likes her. And she must like him, too!"

Inside Sierra's heart, another voice filled her with doubt and anxiety, asking, *Sierra, do you know what you're doing?*

Chapter 2

*J*UST AS THEY APPROACHED THE REST OF THE group at the picnic tables, Sierra conveniently let go of Randy's hand to adjust her ponytail, a task that required both hands. She hoped no one had noticed them holding hands. They would all tease her, and Wesley would be the worst. She had never had a boyfriend before—not that Randy was one, she reminded herself— but to start acting like that now, in front of her whole family, would qualify her for endless teasing later.

"There you are," Sierra's mom said, looking up with a serving spoon in her hand. "We're ready to eat. Howard? We're all here. Would you pray for us?"

"Sure. Why don't we all hold hands?"

Randy reached for Sierra's hand as the group formed a circle. She had to admit that it felt nice and warm and comforting. Randy had rough hands, from working as a gardener. He had built up a nice little business mowing lawns for 12 regular customers. In Portland this time of year, lawns needed mowing at least once a week, so his business was thriving.

Sierra's brother Gavin took her other hand. As she lowered her head to pray, she noticed the pleased look on Amy's face across the circle. She was, of course, holding hands with Wes.

When Dad closed in a group-echoed "Amen," Gavin let go of Sierra's hand and headed for the front of the food line. But Randy kept hold of her hand and gave it a squeeze.

Now Sierra definitely felt embarrassed. If she let go, Randy would think she was being rude. If she kept holding hands, someone would notice. She wondered why Randy wasn't embarrassed to have his parents see them holding hands like she was. With a half-hearted squeeze back, she let go and said, "Do you want me to get you something to drink?"

Oh no! I'm starting to sound like Amy! Sierra thought in horror.

"Sure," Randy said. "Coke, if any is left. I'll grab you some chicken."

"And lots of my mom's potato salad," Sierra added, heading for the ice chest. Reaching her hand into the cold ice, Sierra couldn't help but compare slipping her hand into Randy's strong grip and dipping her hand into the ice chest. She had never noticed before how sensitive hands could be. *All sorts of feelings at my fingertips,* Sierra thought ruefully.

"I like Randy," a voice beside her said softly. It was Sierra's sister-in-law, Katrina. She had on a sunflower-print jumper and wore her thin hair straight around her face. Katrina had a gentle, couldn't-hurt-a-fly look. Sierra had always liked her but had never felt especially close to her. Perhaps it was because Sierra had been only 12 when Katrina married Cody. They had been high school sweethearts and married the week after they graduated. Sierra couldn't imagine herself being ready to marry *anyone* a year from now.

"Are you two going together?" Katrina asked.

"Going together?" Sierra echoed.

Katrina smiled and divulged her secret. "I saw you holding hands. I thought maybe you were going together."

"No, we're buddies," Sierra said calmly. "Just friends." She dredged up a can of ginger ale and wondered why no Cokes were left. "Do you know if any Cokes are in that other ice chest?"

"I don't know," Katrina said. "Are you trying to change the subject?"

Suddenly, Amy stood in front of them. "She always changes the subject when the topic is Randy."

"I do not," Sierra said, plunging her hand back into the ice chest and fishing for a Coke.

Amy gave Katrina a knowing look by raising her dark eyebrows and pulling up the corners of her mouth. "He's crazy about her, but she's not willing to admit how totally crazy she is about him."

"It's not like that, Amy, and you know it."

"The question is," Katrina said, looking Sierra straight in the eyes, "do you like him?"

Sierra looked away. Though she liked the attention

from Randy, she didn't like Katrina's interest in her love life.

"Sure. Everybody likes Randy. He's a great guy. Oh, good. Here's a Coke. Gotta go."

She turned on her heels and delivered the icy soda to Randy. He was still waiting in line and hadn't dished up any food for them yet. As usual, he'd let everyone in the world get in line ahead of him.

"You need to be more aggressive in this family," Sierra told him. "Everybody else sure is. Start reaching, or you'll go hungry." She stretched her arm across the table and grabbed two paper plates. Within minutes the plates were loaded with food, and they were ready to chow down.

Sierra found two seats at the picnic table next to Granna Mae, who was sipping hot coffee from one of her favorite china cups. Granna Mae always drank from a china cup, and the family had gotten used to packing one of her cups and saucers whenever they picnicked.

Granna Mae returned the rose-painted cup to the matching saucer and said, "Hello, Paul. How are you today?"

Sierra bit the inside of her lip.

"I'm Randy. Paul's the one who went to Scotland." Randy shot a sympathetic look at Sierra. He had been around her family enough to see Granna Mae when her mind slipped into a haze like this, and he knew it was best not to try to force the issue. "How's the chicken?"

"Well, dear, I haven't tried it yet. But I do like this fruit salad." Granna Mae speared a chunk of watermelon and held it up. With a quizzical look on her soft face, she asked him, "Rather sweet for this time of year, don't you think?"

"Very sweet," Randy agreed. "Great watermelon."

Wes stuck one of his long legs under the picnic table across from Sierra and plopped down his plate. Before he sat down, he looked at Sierra's plate and said, "Have a little potato salad, why don't you?" His plate held three times the amount of potato salad she had on hers.

"Look who's talking!" she retorted.

"Hey, I've missed Mom's home cooking."

As Wes sat down, Amy slid into the place beside him.

"I thought my family was a bunch of big eaters," Amy said, making herself comfortable. "But now I think you Jensens could out-eat a Degrassi any day. At least this one could." She turned toward Wes with a smile of admiration. Amy's long dark hair hung down her back in a loose pony-tail. Thin curls danced around her face, complimenting her molasses eyes. She was a striking young woman.

"And who's this?" Granna Mae asked.

"That's Amy," Sierra said, leaning close to her grand-mother. "You remember my friend Amy. She was over a couple of nights ago for dinner."

"Oh, yes. The pork chops. I told Emma not to use onions when she cooked them." Granna Mae shook her head and took another bite of fruit salad. "She's always using onions. Onions, onions on everything. Even on pork chops. Can you imagine?"

"Actually," Amy said cautiously. "We had spaghetti the night I was over. And who's Emma?"

Sierra leaned back and shook her head, signaling to Amy there was no point in trying to enter Granna Mae's foggy world, nor would it help to try to coax Granna Mae back into theirs.

"So, Randy," Wes said, a half-devoured drumstick in his hand, "are you going on this backpacking trip Sierra's been talking about?"

"I plan to, if I can finish all my yards."

"I'm going," Amy said brightly. "Why don't you come with us, Wes?"

"I'm not in high school anymore."

"So? Come as a counselor. A trail guide. Assistant to the youth pastor. Why not have some fun this summer? After all, you don't have a job yet."

"Oh, thanks for the gentle reminder, 'Mom.' " Wes rolled his eyes.

"Come on, Sierra. Tell him it'll be fun."

"It'll be fun," Sierra said.

"Randy?" Amy asked, looking for more support.

"It'll be fun, Wes," Randy echoed.

"You two sound real convincing," Wes noted.

"Speaking of fun," Sierra said, "why don't you come with us tonight, Amy? We're serving dinner at the Highland House."

"Thanks, but we're having a big dinner for my dad tonight at home. And you changed the subject again, Sierra. Seems to be your specialty lately."

One of the things Sierra liked about Amy was her persistence—as long as Amy was on a personal mission for some worthy cause, that is. But when Sierra was the object of Amy's mission, she didn't like it one bit.

Amy didn't let up on Wes or on Sierra. On Monday afternoon, Amy came by the house on her way to work. Mrs. Jensen let her in and sent her upstairs to Sierra's room.

It was a big house. Granna Mae had lived in this Victorian two-story since 1915 when her husband built it. Sierra's family had moved here from northern California in January to keep an eye on Granna Mae. And Sierra and Tawni were given the large bedroom at the top of the stairs.

Amy tapped on the bedroom door and walked in. "Hi. I only have about 10 minutes before I have to be at my uncle's restaurant, but I was dying to find out how things went with Randy last night at the Highland House."

"What do you mean?"

"Sierra, come on! I saw you guys when you left the park—holding hands and looking so sweet and cute. He even opened the car door for you."

"So?"

"So, it looks like the beginning of a summer romance to me. What happened after the Highland House? Did he kiss you?"

"Of course not! Amy, how many times do I have to tell you? We're just friends." Sierra stuck a pair of rolled up socks into her dresser drawer and returned to the pile of clothes on her bed. "Nothing happened last night. We left the picnic, went to the Highland House, helped serve dinner, and cleaned up."

"And nothing happened after that?" Amy asked.

"No. He drove me home, came inside, and watched TV for a while with my brothers. I came upstairs, wrote a letter to Christy, and went to bed."

"I don't believe you," Amy said, plopping down on Tawni's now vacant bed. "That isn't the way to catch a boyfriend."

"I'm not trying to catch a boyfriend."

"Obviously," Amy said dryly. She glanced around the room. "What's different here? Something is different."

"Tawni's gone, and so is all her frilly stuff."

"No, it's not just that. This room is looking, well . . . uncluttered. I've never seen your side of the room cleaned up before. And look at you! If I'm not mistaken, you're actually putting clothes away."

"Yes, I am," Sierra said, carrying a bunch of clothes on hangers over to the closet and hanging them in the empty space.

"What's come over you? You feeling okay?"

"I decided to clean my room, that's all. It's a big room, and it looks better picked up."

"This is not like you."

"Maybe it is," Sierra said, sitting cross-legged on the bed next to Amy. "Maybe now that Tawni's gone, my true self will sprout in all kinds of ways. Like maybe deep down I'm really a tidy person. But I never explored that because my whole life I had a neat-freak sister for a roommate, and she kept things spotless enough for both of us. Now, maybe, I'm finding out who I really am. Do you know what I'm saying?"

"You're weird."

"Oh, come on. You have older sisters. Didn't you change some when they moved out?"

"No."

"Not at all?"

Amy shook her head. "I was and always will be the baby of the family. Nothing changed when they left. Which reminds me, instead of fixing dinner at my house on Wednesday night, can we fix it over here?"

"Why?" Sierra was surprised that Amy was willing to make any adjustments to their dinner plan. For almost a month, Amy had been devising a scheme to get Drake to come to her house for dinner. Sierra had agreed to invite Randy so it could be a foursome. They had planned and scheduled and rescheduled. Finally, everything was set for this Wednesday night. Why would Amy want to change locations?

"I thought it would be more fun over here," Amy said. "It's so quiet and boring at my house. My parents will lock themselves in the TV room upstairs, and I don't know, it just wouldn't be as lively as things always seem to be around here."

Sierra began to get the picture. "You mean Wes won't be around if we have it at your house."

Amy innocently blinked her thick lashes at Sierra. "Why did you say that? Why would I want Wes to be around when I'm on a date with Drake?"

"It was just a thought," Sierra said. "We wouldn't be

able to make the dinner fancy here. My brothers would get into everything and join us at the table. If you want a quiet dinner for four like you've planned all along, we should have it at your house."

"Okay, okay. If you say so." Amy glanced at her watch and forced herself to get up. "I have to go. By the way, is Wes home?"

Sierra grinned at her not-so-subtle friend. "Nope. He's out job hunting."

"Well, tell him I hope he doesn't find a job until after the backpacking trip. Okay? Tell him I said that."

"I will, Amy. See you later."

Amy scurried out of the room, closing the door behind her. Sierra lay back on Tawni's bed and stared at the ceiling. Its uneven ivory stucco presented an interesting pattern. To Sierra, it looked like clumps of clouds floating in a winter sky, untouched by the earth below, unhindered by the heavens above.

That's how Sierra wanted to be. Light and free and unhindered. Why would she want a boyfriend? Or want things with Randy to be any different from what they were right now? Warm and nice and uncomplicated. Just friends. Sierra decided she wanted to float through this summer the way she had managed to breeze through almost everything else in life. Like a cloud. That's what she wanted to be—a cloud.

Chapter 3

"**M**OM, I'M LEAVING FOR WORK NOW,**"** Sierra called out the back door the next morning.

Her mother was bent over in the garden, stringing up green beans. She stood and motioned for Sierra to wait a minute. Stepping cautiously over the rows of strawberries, her mom jogged to the back door. Sharon Jensen was a slim, energetic woman who seemed to enjoy life and her six children to the fullest. She loved it when people told her she was too young to be a grandmother, which she had been for three years now, ever since the appearance of Sierra's nephew, Tyler.

Everyone told Sierra she looked like her mom except that her hair was blond and her mother's was light brown. They also said she had her mom's figure. Sierra had never liked her tomboy shape, though. Compared with her shapely sister, she felt unattractive. But every now and then, when she saw her mom like this, looking cute in her shorts and a sleeveless shirt that showed off her sunburned shoulders, Sierra hoped she would turn out just like her.

"Will you stop by the store on the way home for me? There's a list and some money on the counter. You'll be home by six, won't you?"

"I should be. I get off at five."

"Good," her mom said, dabbing her sweaty nose with the back of her gloved hand. "Gavin has a friend coming for dinner. Do you know if Randy's coming?"

"Why would he?"

"Well, he's been stopping by at dinnertime a lot lately. I just wondered if he had said anything to you."

"No, I'm afraid I can't ever make predictions about Randy."

"He knows he's always welcome. There will be plenty if he shows up."

"Okay. Well, I'm off. See you at six."

Sierra grabbed the list and cash and headed for the '79 Volkswagen Rabbit parked out front. She slipped into the car and puttered down the street to her job at Mama Bear's. Parking in the lot behind the bakery, she walked in the back door at exactly 10:00.

The day flew by, as every day had since Mrs. Kraus installed a frozen yogurt machine. She had advertised in front of the shop with a giant yogurt cone perched atop the sign that read "Mama Bear's Cinnamon Rolls." As a result, the clientele had immediately grown to include neighborhood kids and the uniformed employees from the medical center a block away.

When Sierra started this job in late winter, she had been busy making specialty coffees all day. Now it was swirled yogurt cones. Mrs. Kraus had talked about adding a small hot pot for chocolate coating so they could offer dipped cones. Sierra and several other employees had begged her to reconsider. The yogurt was sticky and messy enough without adding quick drying chocolate to the menu.

Sierra was preparing to leave that afternoon when Mrs. Kraus approached her with the schedule in her hand. "Let me get this straight," she said, chewing on the end of her pencil. "You'll be working your regular hours this week, but you'll be gone next week. Right?"

Mrs. Kraus was a short, round, good-natured woman who had a thing about all her employees wearing matching aprons. She had changed the staff aprons twice since Sierra had started there. This week they were wearing hot-pink ones with little ice cream cones and cherries sprinkled across the fabric.

Hanging up her apron, Sierra looked over her shoulder at Mrs. Kraus. "Yes, I'm going backpacking, remember? I can still work my regular hours next Saturday, though."

"Backpacking? How brave of you, dear! Where are you going?"

"Some place in Washington State. It's not far."

"Sleeping on cold dirt, eating dehydrated rations, and hiking until your legs ache. . . . My, how wonderful it is to be young!"

Sierra laughed. "We have tents. And it's not exactly strenuous. It'll be fun."

"If you say so, dear. Now, you leave on Monday." She

was busy writing and erasing as she spoke. "Then can you work Friday of this week from noon to nine? I'm trying out the later hours on weekends during the summer, and I've been in a dither to get the time covered. Can you work this Friday?"

"I guess so. I usually help out serving dinner at the Highland House on Fridays, but I think Uncle Mac will understand." Sierra ran her hands under the faucet, trying to wash off the stickiness.

Ever since she and Randy had volunteered at the Highland House as a service project for school, they had continued to go back and assist where needed. The Highland House ran an after-school program for kids and offered job-search aid to their parents. The center also fed and provided beds for dozens of homeless people each night. Sierra was preparing her own version of a vacation Bible school for the kids at the Highland House and planned to start the morning program in July.

Uncle Mac, the director, was thrilled to have Sierra working there. He had taken a special interest in her, not just because of her initiative in starting the Bible school program, but also because Tawni's new boyfriend, Jeremy, was Uncle Mac's nephew. As a matter of fact, the Paul who had moved to Scotland was Jeremy's brother. Sierra was sure it was all divine intervention.

"Okay. The schedule is all set," Mrs. Kraus said. "I'll see you Thursday morning."

"See you then," Sierra said, giving a wave and quickly stepping out the back door before they started to chat about something else. Mrs. Kraus was fun to talk to, but Sierra knew that if they got started, she would be there for another hour.

To her surprise, Drake was leaning on her car, with his arms folded across his broad chest. His dark hair contained glints of amber in the afternoon sun. His square jaw was set firmly, and his eyes were on Sierra.

"To what do I owe the pleasure of this surprise, Mr. Drake?" Sierra listened to herself, not sure where her brain had come up with such a coy remark. Maybe she had been watching too many black-and-white movies late at night.

Drake's full name was Anton Francisco Drake. He never apologized for his sophisticated name, but preferred that everyone simply call him "Drake," since it didn't seem one could glean a usable nickname from Anton or Francisco. And just like his name, Drake, the six-foot-two star athlete, was one of a kind.

"I'm killing time. I left my car at the shop across the street and thought I'd stop by to see you while I waited for them to fix the muffler."

"Oh, well, I just finished work, and I have to run to the store for my mom."

"Mind if I come along?"

Sierra was sure her face reflected surprise. "Fine."

She climbed into the car and leaned over to unlock the passenger door. Drake folded his tall frame into the small vehicle and immediately tried to scoot the seat back.

"You have enough room?" Sierra asked.

"Just enough," he said.

"I think Amy's working tonight," Sierra said as she started the car. "Have you seen her much lately?" Sierra knew the answer but wanted to see how Drake would respond.

"Not much," Drake said, adjusting the seat some more. "She seems to be working or at your house whenever I call her."

"Oh, I see," Sierra said with a tease in her voice. "So you figured if you tracked me down, Amy wouldn't be far away."

"Actually," Drake said, "I wanted to see you."

Sierra felt her heart pounding as her car took the bump into the Safeway parking lot. Why would Drake say that? Could he tell that Amy wasn't interested in him anymore? Or was this Drake's method of moving from girl to girl and never letting anyone think he was going with a particular person?

Sierra didn't respond to Drake's comment but pulled into a parking spot and turned off the engine. "I have only a few things on the list. You want to come in with me?"

"Sure. This is much better than reading auto shop magazines."

"When will your car be ready?"

"Hopefully, by 6:30," Drake said, letting her walk in front of him through the automatic doors and into the air-conditioned store. The blast of cool air felt good to Sierra and helped to clear her head.

He's only killing time. Don't read anything into his com-

ment. Drake is just being friendly, she thought.

It felt strange walking up and down the aisles with Drake pushing the cart. Sierra made herself busy as she read the list, compared prices on pickle jars, and then checked the list again. She couldn't remember the last time she had felt so nervous.

"I think that's everything," she said, finally making eye contact with him. All through the store, she had felt his eyes on her.

Drake steered the cart into the 10-items-or-less lane and helped her unload the groceries.

"Make a guess," he said.

"A guess?"

"How much do you think this will add up to?"

"I don't know. Under 20 dollars I hope, because that's all I have."

"I think it will be 11 dollars and 67 cents. Go ahead. You guess."

Sierra looked away from his good-natured smile and mentally priced the items rolling past her. "Nine dollars and 17 cents," she said.

"I don't think so." Drake's dark eyes sparkled.

The total rang up as $14.92.

"Fourteen ninety-two?" they both echoed.

"What did I buy?" Sierra asked.

"Hey, fourteen ninety-two," Drake repeated. "Great year for sailing the ocean blue. Just ask Columbus."

He grinned. Sierra shook her head at his joke and handed over the 20-dollar bill.

Drake carried the bag to the car for her. "I think it was the tomatoes," he said. "They're not really in season yet."

"And how do you know this, Mr. Tomato Expert?"

Drake shrugged and placed the groceries on the backseat. "Our backyard is full of tomato plants, and they still have little green balls on them, not big, fat red ones. That's how I know. Doesn't take a rocket scientist."

Sierra settled into the driver's seat and glanced at her reflection in the rearview mirror before Drake wedged himself in. Her cheeks carried the blush of pink she felt inside.

"You mind dropping me off at the auto shop on your way home?" Drake asked. "Or, actually, would you mind taking me there and waiting? They weren't sure they could fix it tonight."

Sierra waited as Drake entered the small shop and stood at the counter, talking to the mechanic. A thousand swirling thoughts, like confetti in the wind, blew through Sierra's mind.

Why is he being so nice? I never dreamed Drake would be interested in me. This is so flattering! I can't believe he stopped to see me.

Drake jogged back to Sierra's car, looking like a football player entering the stadium and anticipating the crowd's roar of approval. Sierra rolled down her window. He leaned over, resting his muscled arms on her door.

"Well, it looks as if I'll have to come back tomorrow. They're not finished with it yet."

"Do you want me to give you a ride home?" Sierra asked.

Drake was so close to her that his face was only inches away. Before she realized what was happening, he reached over and, with a thick finger, brushed something off her cheek.

Sierra's hand instinctively reached for the same spot and began to wipe her cheek. "What was it?"

"A gnat or something."

"Probably a mosquito," Sierra said. "They're already coming after me. Mosquitoes love me."

"You know what they say. Mosquitoes only go for sweet blood."

"Oh, really?" Sierra said. "My mom says it's because I don't take enough vitamin B."

Drake sauntered over to the passenger side and got back in the car. Sierra felt herself blushing again.

What is wrong with me? I'm rambling about mosquitoes and vitamins while Drake is sitting in my car!

"So, where to?" Sierra forced herself to ask calmly as she started up the engine.

"That depends," Drake said. "Are you interested in going out to dinner?"

Chapter 4

*S*IERRA AND DRAKE WALKED SIDE BY SIDE UP THE front steps of her home. She opened the door, and he carried in the bag of groceries.

"Anybody home?"

There was no answer. They went into the kitchen and heard voices coming from the backyard. Sounds always carried from the deck into the kitchen like a funnel.

Sierra motioned for Drake to place the grocery sack on the kitchen counter and peeked out the window over the sink. Mr. Jensen stood in front of the barbecue, swatting at the cloud of smoke with his spatula. Granna Mae reclined on a patio lounge chair under the shade of one of the huge oak trees that lined the backyard. Gavin and his friend were taunting Brutus with a stick, holding it up and trying to entice him to jump. Mrs. Jensen stood by the patio table with a glass of iced tea in her hand, talking with Wes. Sierra's eight-year-old brother Dillon was sitting at the table, ready to eat as usual. Sierra felt like an eavesdropper, spying on her family through the window.

"Come on," Sierra said, leading Drake outside. "They're all out back."

"There she is," Wes said, spotting Sierra as she stepped onto the deck.

"Hi, everybody! This is Drake, a friend of mine from school. Mom, do you mind if we have one more for dinner?"

"Of course not. How are you, Drake?"

"Fine, thanks. I appreciate your letting me crash your barbecue like this."

"No problem," Sierra's dad said from the grill. "We always have plenty. You're welcome anytime. The burgers will be ready in about three minutes."

"Oh!" Her mom turned to Sierra. "Did you pick up those items at the store? I need to cut up the tomatoes and get the condiments on the table." She disappeared inside the kitchen.

"Time to eat, Granna Mae," Sierra said, going over and giving her snoozing grandma a kiss on the cheek. "You hungry?"

"Oh, goodness me," she said, looking up at Sierra. "When did you get back?"

"Just a few minutes ago. Are you ready for some dinner?"

"Well, tell me about your trip. Did you have a nice time?" Granna Mae smoothed back her hair and shifted in the lounge chair.

"I had a very nice time," Sierra said, playing along and offering her a hand up from the chair. "Come meet my friend Drake."

They walked arm in arm to the table, where Granna Mae stopped to take a good look at Drake. She smiled cordially and found her place at the table. Sierra felt relieved that Granna Mae didn't say anything more. Drake might not understand that Granna Mae's mind was fuzzy.

Drake and Sierra sat next to each other. All eyes seemed to be on Drake, waiting for him to speak. Sierra felt proud and confident. It wasn't every day she had someone important like Drake as her guest.

"Heads up!" her dad said. "Burgers coming through."

"They smell great," Drake said, rubbing his hands in anticipation.

"I better start you off with two," Mr. Jensen offered.

"If you're sure you have enough."

"We always have extra," Dillon piped up. "That's 'cause Randy eats with us a lot. Do you know Randy?"

"Sure do."

"Randy is Sierra's boyfriend."

"He is not!" Sierra spouted. "I mean, you know." She looked at Drake and then back at Dillon. "Randy's my friend, not my boyfriend."

"Then how come you hold hands with him?"

Sierra felt her face beginning to burn. She suspected her brother was old enough to know that his words would embarrass and upset her, and he seemed to enjoy his role as the pesky little brother.

Just then her mother stepped onto the deck with a tray of condiments. Her eyes were on Sierra, and in a flash

Sierra knew why. Randy was right behind her. They had heard every word in the kitchen.

"You're just in time," her dad said, saving Sierra from the awkward moment. "You hungry, Randy?"

"He's always hungry," Gavin said.

"Join us," Mr. Jensen said.

"Hey, Drake," Randy said. "How's it going?"

He ambled over to the patio table, still wearing his grass-stained work clothes. Sitting next to Dillon, he acted like one of the family. He appeared unaffected by what Sierra had said while he was in the kitchen.

Sierra fidgeted, shifting her glance from Drake to Randy.

"How are you doin'?" Drake asked Randy.

"Good. I got two more offers today for lawns on Belmont Street. You sure you don't want to join me in the yard business this summer?"

"I'm locked in," Drake said. "I told my dad I'd work for him all summer."

Sierra watched the two of them share the bottle of ketchup and information about their summer jobs. Apparently, they didn't mind sharing their relationship with Sierra as well. So why was she flustered?

Dinner progressed at its normal pace around the Jensen table with lots of lively conversation, lots of food, and not a shred of evidence that anyone other than Sierra thought it strange that she had two dinner guests.

She eagerly volunteered to help clear dishes and serve the dessert. With full hands, she followed her mother into the house. From the kitchen window, she could hear Wes asking if anyone wanted to join him in a game of basketball after dessert.

"Is this normal?" Sierra asked her mom, turning away from the window.

"Is what normal?"

"Having two guys over for dinner."

"Feels normal to me. How does it feel to you?"

"Weird," Sierra said with a sigh, leaning against the counter. "I was so flattered when Drake stopped by to see me at work. I thought maybe he was, well, you know . . . interested in me or something."

"Did he give you that impression?"

"Yes. Sort of. I think. Oh, I don't know."

Mom pulled the ice cream from the freezer and began to scoop it into the line of bowls she had placed on the counter. "The strawberries are in the fridge, Sierra. Could you get them for me?"

"You know what I'm realizing?" Sierra said as she took out the large bowl of fresh strawberries. "I don't know much about guys. Tawni used to call me a late bloomer, and as much as I hate to admit it, I think she was right. This is all new to me. I mean, why would Drake come to see me at work when Amy is the one who's interested in him?"

"Easy," her mother replied. "Because you're not interested in him."

"So that makes me a challenge or something?"

"Something like that. Here, scoop the strawberries on top, will you?"

"But the thing is, I am interested in Drake. At least I think I could be if I knew he liked me."

"And what about Randy?"

"That's the weird part. I don't want Randy to go away just because Drake is here."

Mrs. Jensen glanced out the window and said, "Oh, I don't think Randy is going anywhere."

"But what about Amy, Mom? We're supposed to make dinner for Drake and Randy at her house tomorrow night. Drake is her date, and Randy is mine. Except now I feel like Amy would be mad if she knew Drake was over here tonight."

"Why?"

"Because she likes Drake."

"Does she?"

Sierra felt even more frustrated than before she had started talking with her mom. She was getting nowhere, and all her questions were only being answered with more questions.

"Aren't you going to tell me how a good little Christian daughter should handle all this?" she pleaded.

"No."

"No?"

Her mother put down the ice cream scoop and gently cupped Sierra's chin in her hand. "I've been doing that for 16 years, honey. It's time for you to show me what you've got. Show me what you're made of."

"Oh great!" Sierra said as Mrs. Jensen went back to scooping up the last two bowls. "You're leaving me to figure this out all by myself."

"You're never completely by yourself," her mom said. "You know that."

"Yes," Sierra said, topping off the last bowl with a generous mound of strawberries. "Aren't you going to quote me your favorite saying? 'Mothers couldn't be everywhere so that's why God sent the Holy Spirit.'"

"You *have* been listening." Her mom placed the bowls on a tray and headed for the back door. She turned to give Sierra an over-the-shoulder smile. It was a gleeful grin, like the smile her mother had given her last Christmas when Sierra opened up the present from her parents. It was a plane ticket to England for the missions trip she went on in January.

"Without a doubt, this is going to be your best summer yet, Sierra. I just know it."

Sierra watched her mother disappear and listened to the comforting slap of the screen door as it closed behind her. It seemed she and her mother had officially entered the next level in their relationship. An invisible door had closed on what was, and a whole new world had opened up on what would be.

Chapter 5

THE BASKETBALL GAME IN SIERRA'S DRIVEWAY lasted until nearly 10:00. Drake, Randy, and Wes hogged the ball, but Sierra and her dad both elbowed their way into the game and managed to score a few points. In many ways, it felt like any other summer night in Sierra's childhood. The sky stayed light until 9:30, crickets played their summer symphony in the cool green grass, happy shouts came from Gavin and Dillon amid eager barks from Brutus, and Wes and a bunch of his friends worked up a sweat and called out friendly insults. Only tonight, the guys in the driveway were Sierra's friends, not Wesley's.

Strange feelings surrounded Sierra all night. Her mom might have been confident that Sierra would figure out these relationships, but Sierra wasn't so sure. There were so many undefined pieces. Was Drake interested in her? Was Amy still interested in Drake? What would it be like tomorrow night at Amy's house if Drake was Amy's date, but he paid more attention to Sierra?

"I better get going," Randy finally said. "I have to start

work early tomorrow morning. What time are we meeting at Amy's?"

"Is that tomorrow night?" Drake asked, holding the basketball in the crook of his arm and wiping his chin with the front of his T-shirt.

Sierra sat on the grass by the driveway–basketball court. Her legs were stretched out and crossed at the ankles. Leaning back on her hands, she tilted her head and asked, "Do you guys still want to have the dinner?"

"Yes," they said in unison.

"Of course," Randy added. "Why? Are you and Amy having second thoughts about trying to feed us?"

"No, not at all." Sierra made a mental note that Randy and Drake acted as if nothing were unusual about both of them being here tonight. They both actually seemed eager to get together tomorrow. What could that mean?

"Okay," Sierra said, getting up and brushing off the seat of her jeans. "Six o'clock at Amy's. And remember, it's fancy." She noticed Wes standing to the side with a smirk on his face. "What's so funny?" she challenged him.

"Nothing. Sounds like you'll have a lot of fun." His grin got wider.

"Why don't you join us?" Drake said, tossing the ball to Wes. "I'm sure Amy wouldn't mind."

Does Drake know about Amy's crush on Wes? Sierra wondered.

"Thanks, but that's okay. Maybe another time."

"Okay," Drake responded; then he turned to Randy. "Hey, Randy, can you give me a ride home?"

"Sure. You ready to go?"

"Yep." Drake looked at Sierra and smiled. "Thanks for dinner, Sierra."

"Yeah," Randy said with a smile. "It was great."

They headed for Randy's truck. At the curb, they both stopped to wave good-bye.

"See you at Amy's," Randy called out.

The minute the truck pulled away from the curb and started down the street, Wes let out a hearty chuckle.

"What?" Sierra demanded. They were the only ones out front now, and it seemed that the night air had suddenly turned chilly. She hadn't noticed it while they were playing basketball.

"You are going to break some hearts, little sister!" Wes spun the basketball on his finger and caught it before it toppled to the ground.

She couldn't tell if he was teasing or complimenting her.

"How old are you going to be this November?"

"Seventeen," she said firmly. "You know that."

Wes's grin pushed up the crinkles in the corners of his eyes.

"Why is that so funny?" Sierra said, annoyed.

"It's not. It's just that I guess I didn't see it coming. Little Sierra all grown up with a line of eligible bachelors at her front door. I remember when the phone started to ring off the hook for Tawni."

"Only she was 13, not 16, right?"

"Something like that." Wes sidled up to Sierra and put

a sweaty, smelly arm around her shoulder, giving her a squeeze. "Now it's your turn, Golden Girl. Go easy on Randy though, will you? I kind of like the guy."

"So? Who asked you?" Sierra said, ducking out of his hug.

"No need to ask. My expert opinions are always available free of charge. And it's my opinion that Randy is more your speed."

"Oh, yeah?" Sierra said, playfully tapping the ball out of his hand. "And exactly what speed is that?"

The ball bounced through Wes's fingertips and rolled down the driveway and into the street.

Wes crossed his arms, attempting to look threatening. "Go get the ball."

"I'm not your dog. You get the ball." Sierra stood on the driveway, hands on her hips, chin jutted out in defiance, waiting for her brother to tackle her, rough up her hair, throw grass in her face, or hoist her over his shoulder and cart her to the street, where he would make her pick up the ball.

Wes looked her over slowly, as if trying to decide which tactic would work best. Suddenly, a different expression washed over his face, a look of tenderness rather than teasing. Then he cleared his throat and said in a serious voice, "If you ever need someone to talk to, about guys or whatever—especially now that Tawni's gone—I'll be around all summer. You know you can talk to me, don't you?"

Those were the last words Sierra expected from her

brother's lips. Had she somehow walked through an invisible door with Wesley the same way she had entered a new level in her relationship with her mom?

"Sure. Thanks," Sierra said, feeling as if that was the expected response.

Wes smiled and said, "I'll get the ball this time."

He hustled down to the street, and Sierra went inside, shaking her head. She climbed the stairs, trying to make sense of all that was happening in her life.

Is there a sign on my forehead that says, "Treat me like an adult"? Or does everyone believe the door to my social life has swung open because Drake showed up tonight?

Whatever it was, she didn't understand the change. And it certainly came as a surprise.

The next morning Sierra was in for another surprise when she came downstairs to breakfast. Her plan was to eat something and then call Amy to fill her in on the events of the night before.

She had carefully thought through her words in the shower. "Amy," she rehearsed, "I need to tell you that Drake came to my house last night for dinner. I want to know how you feel about that and whether you still want to make dinner for the guys tonight, because if you're not interested in Drake anymore, then . . ." Her words froze every time she got to the part about Drake. Certainly, a banana and a bowl of Golden Grahams would bring her thinking into focus, she decided.

But when Sierra stepped into the kitchen, she found Amy sitting at the kitchen counter, crying behind a barricade of cereal boxes. Wes stood at the kitchen sink, a glass of orange juice in his hand. They both turned to look at Sierra when she walked in.

"What's wrong?" Sierra asked quickly, looking first at Wes, then at Amy.

With a sniff and a deep breath, Amy said, "My parents decided to have a big yelling match this morning. My dad stomped out all mad, and my mom ran to her room and locked the door. I hate it when they do this."

Sierra sat down next to Amy and slipped her arm around her shoulders. "I'm sure it'll work out. Doesn't it usually blow over in an hour or two?"

"Usually," Amy said with a sniff. "But I don't know what to do about our dinner tonight. I don't want to have all you guys over if they're going to fight again."

"You probably should stay clear," Wes said, getting his two-cents' worth into the conversation. "It might be better not to add any complications to the evening in case your parents need time to talk when your dad comes home from work. Why don't you guys reschedule your dinner?"

"We've already rescheduled four times!" Amy said, getting up and going over to the side counter to grab a napkin from the basket. She wiped her eyes and blew her nose. "I guess we should cancel the whole thing and forget it. I'll tell my uncle we don't need the lobsters tonight after all."

"Lobsters?" Wes noted.

"We can have it here," Sierra heard herself saying.

"Are you sure your parents wouldn't mind?" Amy asked, her expression brightening.

Sierra knew Amy hadn't planned for her parents to quarrel. She wasn't trying to set things up so that Wes would be a part of their fancy dinner. But it sure was working out conveniently.

"I'm sure it'll be fine," Sierra said. "I'll call Drake and Randy to tell them. Do you still want it to be at six?"

"Sure. I can pick up the lobsters anytime this afternoon. We still have to shop for the salad and rolls and decide on some kind of vegetable. What do you like?"

"Zucchini," Wes jumped in. "The way Mom makes it."

"She didn't ask you," Sierra said, tossing her brother a "get lost" look.

"What are we going to have for dessert?" Amy asked.

The doorbell rang, and Wes left to answer it, giving Sierra the opportunity to try to have her heart-to-heart talk with Amy.

Sierra took a deep breath. "I need to ask you something. How are you feeling about Drake?"

Amy gave her a funny look.

"I mean do you still like him?"

"Of course I still like him. I've always liked Drake. Who wouldn't?"

This wasn't the answer Sierra expected.

"Why?" Amy asked.

"I thought you weren't that interested in him anymore."

Amy shook her head. "I'm totally interested in him!

Drake isn't crazy about me, but I thought if he got to know me better, he would change his mind. That's why I wanted to do this dinner. Why do you ask?"

Sierra poured herself a bowl of cereal. "I need to tell you something."

She dipped her spoon into the bowl and tried to find a good opening line. Maybe Amy wouldn't care that Drake had spent last evening at Sierra's. *Yeah, right!* Sierra thought, shuddering. *What if this is the end of our friendship?*

"Amy, listen to what I say and don't get mad, okay?"

"Why would I get mad?"

Sierra knew she hadn't done anything wrong. Drake had sought her out, not the other way around. And there was nothing unusual about inviting a friend home for dinner. So why did she feel guilty?

Just then Wes walked back in with a UPS package in his hand. "Do you know if Mom is still around?"

"I don't know," Sierra said.

Gavin burst in the back door, laughing and running through the house. Dillon entered right behind him with a squirt gun in his hand.

"Hey guys," Wes said in a booming voice, "take it outside."

"Okay, *Dad*." They chased each other around the table and out the back door.

"We can't talk in here," Sierra said, exasperated. "Let's go upstairs. You know, maybe we should postpone the dinner again. It'll be like this the whole time around here."

"No it won't," Wes said. "I'll take everyone out for pizza. You guys can have the whole place to yourselves."

Amy's face clouded over. "You don't have to go anywhere, Wes."

The phone rang, and as Wes reached for it, he said, "Yes, I think I do."

"Come on, Aim. Let's go up to my room."

"Sierra," Wes called as they headed toward the hall, "phone. It's Drake."

Chapter 6

S IERRA FROZE.

"Let me talk to him. He probably guessed I'd be over here since I wasn't home," Amy said, reaching to take the phone from Wes's hand and answering with, "Hi."

Wes stepped back and crossed his arms across his chest, amused by the scenario.

"Friday night?" Amy said. "I'd love to! I have to work till nine, so we'd have to go to the late show. What? No, this is Amy." She shot a glance at Sierra. "Who did you think you were talking to?"

Sierra pursed her lips together and looked down at her bare feet. Her heart was pounding like a drum.

"She's right here," Amy said and held out the phone to Sierra.

Tears began to well up in Amy's eyes as she grabbed her purse from the counter and spouted, "I can't believe you didn't tell me, Sierra! Forget the dinner." She brushed past Sierra and marched for the front door.

"Drake?" Sierra said into the receiver. "I'll have to call you back."

"I'm not at home," he said. "I'm at work. You want me to call you?"

"No. I mean yes."

Sierra heard Amy sobbing as she opened the front door.

Her emotions torn in two, Sierra said quickly into the phone, "I don't know, Drake. Whatever."

She hung up the phone and dashed to the front door. Amy was already down the sidewalk, unlocking the door of her Volvo.

"Amy, wait!"

Amy ignored her, got in, and slammed the door. Sierra bolted down the steps and ran to the curb as Amy started the car. She turned the key in the ignition, but nothing happened.

"Amy, we need to talk!" Sierra pounded her fist on the closed passenger window.

Amy ignored her and tried the key again. Nothing.

Sierra noticed the lock was up on the passenger door and quickly opened it before Amy could reach over to lock it. Plopping herself inside, Sierra slammed the door shut.

Amy forced the unresponsive ignition key again, and in a voice filled with anger, she said, "I have nothing to talk to you about!"

"Amy," Sierra said, trying to be calm, "don't do this. Talk to me. It's not what you think."

"Oh really?" Amy turned her tear-streaked face toward Sierra. "Then what is it?"

"It's a misunderstanding, and we need to talk about it."

"No, we don't. Leave me alone!"

"I won't leave you alone," Sierra answered firmly. "I'm going to sit here until you talk to me. You can't walk out when you're mad. You'll never solve anything that way. Look at your parents." As soon as the words popped out of Sierra's mouth, she realized that was the worst thing she could have said.

Oh, when am I ever going to learn to keep my mouth shut?

Amy burst into tears and dropped her forehead onto the steering wheel. Sierra had never heard anyone sob so uncontrollably.

"I'm sorry," Sierra said, cautiously reaching over and placing a hand on Amy's shoulder. "All I'm saying is that you and I need to talk this out."

Amy cried and cried.

Sierra rolled down the window in the stuffy car and waited for Amy to calm down.

Finally, Amy lifted her head from the steering wheel and shouted, "Everyone is deserting me! Everyone I know has turned against me."

"I'm not against you," Sierra said in firm, even words.

"Oh please!" Amy glared at Sierra, her eyes puffy and her cheeks soaked with tears. "You steal my boyfriend and then say you're not against me? You're a liar!"

"I am not a liar, Amy. And I didn't steal your boyfriend. I've been trying to tell you what happened."

"I don't want to hear it."

"Amy," Sierra said, struggling to keep calm. "Don't act like this. Listen to me. Drake took his car in to be fixed yesterday, and then he came over to Mama Bear's right when I was getting off work. He said he was just killing time, so he went to the grocery store with me. Then I took him back to the garage, and they weren't done with his car yet, so I invited him to my house for dinner."

"Oh, that was convenient," Amy said, wiping her cheek with the back of her hand.

"Listen to me, Amy. Randy was there, too. My family was having a barbecue, and afterward we all played basketball. Randy gave Drake a ride home, and that was it."

Amy looked at her skeptically and sniffed loudly. "Randy was there, too?"

"Yes. Randy was there, too. He gave Drake a ride home. Nobody was stealing anybody's boyfriend."

"Why did he come to see you at work instead of me?"

"For one thing, the garage was right across the street. For another, he told me he had tried to call you the last few days, but you were never home."

"Yes I was. He's lying."

"You can't go around accusing everyone of being a liar," Sierra stated firmly. "Look at yourself. You're falling apart over nothing."

"It isn't nothing," Amy said, brushing back her hair and reaching in her purse for a tissue. She blew her nose and blurted through her tears, "My parents are going to get a divorce."

Chapter 7

"**D**O YOU KNOW THAT FOR SURE?**" SIERRA asked. "I mean, have they actually said they're getting a divorce, or are you feeling that way because things were so bad between them this morning?"

"I'm positive," Amy said. "I heard them fighting once a few months ago, and they said they were going to wait until I graduated next year. Then they would sell the house and split everything."

Sierra didn't know what to say.

"The way things are going, I don't think they'll last until the end of the month."

"I'm sorry you're going through all this," Sierra said. "I'm glad you're telling me."

"I probably shouldn't be saying all this." Amy drew in a shaky breath. "I just don't know what to do."

"I don't think you can do anything. Except pray. Pray good and hard. This is something your parents have to work out."

They were silent for a few minutes. Sierra could hear

the morning birds singing their hearts out in the towering trees in the backyard. She remembered a saying she had once seen on a greeting card. "The blue bird does not sing because she has the answer. She sings because she has a song."

"Amy, let's put this morning behind us, okay? I don't have any answers for you. I just want to start fresh."

"You always do that," Amy said, looking Sierra in the eyes for the first time since Sierra had clambered into her car. "You spring back all the time. Don't you ever get depressed?"

"Sure. Sometimes. Everybody does."

Amy pulled her hair away from her face and reached for a ponytail holder hanging from her rearview mirror. With her hair back and her eyes wiped, she faced Sierra with a forced smile. "Okay. Fresh start. I can deal with Drake liking you."

"I never said he liked me."

"Well, Drake is interested enough to call you and ask you to the movies Friday night, in case you hadn't figured that out yet. That makes it a bit awkward for us to fix dinner for the guys tonight and still assume that Drake is my date."

"Why should it be?"

"Sierra! Think about it."

"I never said I'd go to the movies with him. I never gave Drake any indication that I was interested in him."

"But you are, aren't you? I mean, if I hadn't picked up the phone, you would have said yes to the movies, wouldn't you?"

Sierra paused before answering. "I don't know."

"Come on, Sierra. You've always been honest with me. Why can't you tell me the truth now? I can take it. Believe me! After all I've been through this morning, I can take anything."

Sierra let out a deep breath and lifted her thick hair off her clammy neck. How should she answer?

"I don't know how I feel, Amy. I just don't know." She shook her head and looked out the car window.

The front of the Jensen house looked like a picture from a *Better Homes and Gardens* magazine. The wide, wraparound porch was decorated with her mom's baskets of hanging ferns, and along the railing her flower boxes were alive with color. It all seemed so peaceful and inviting. A vivid contrast to the way Sierra felt inside.

"We can't fix dinner tonight," Amy said. "That's for sure."

"I still don't understand why not."

Amy gave her an incredulous look. "Do the math, girl! You would have two dates, and I would have none."

"Why can't we all just be a bunch of friends having dinner together and not divide up into couples?" Sierra suggested. "We're all friends, aren't we? Why do we have to match people up? I hate that."

"Why should you hate that? You're the one with all the male attention at the moment."

"So what do you want to do?" Sierra sighed.

"Nothing. I want to cancel the dinner. I want to go home." Amy paused. She reached for her sunglasses on the dashboard and slipped them on. "No, I don't want to go home. I don't know what I want right now. I just want to get out of here."

"Don't leave mad, Amy."

"I'm not mad." She turned the key in the ignition, and the car started immediately.

"Are you sure?"

"Yes, I'm sure. I'll talk to you later," Amy said.

"Well, call me or come by later or something. I have the whole day free now."

"I'll call you," Amy said. "But you call the guys, okay?"

"Okay," Sierra reluctantly agreed, opening the car door and getting out. "You will call me, right?"

"I told you I would." Amy pulled Sierra's door shut and charged away, making her tires squeal as she sped down the street.

She's still mad, and she's not going to call me, Sierra thought.

With her bare feet nestled in the cool grass, Sierra watched a puff of gray smoke rise from the old Volvo as it turned down the next street. Sierra felt hollow inside. There didn't seem to be any easy answers, no snap decisions that would make everything right and peaceful again.

Why does life have to be so complicated? I should call Drake and tell him I can't go to the movies with him. Then Amy will have nothing to be mad about, Sierra thought. *No, I can't do that. He never actually asked me. He thought he was asking me, but he really only talked to Amy.* Then Sierra had an idea. *What if Randy came with us? No, that's too strange.* She went back and forth. *No, it isn't. Randy's just a buddy. Or is he?*

The nagging little voice inside of Sierra was beginning to make her feel as if she were going crazy, causing her to doubt herself and everyone else.

A large, white delivery van rumbled down the street and pulled up where Amy's car had been, interrupting Sierra's thoughts. The words on the side of the van read, "Bundle of Joy—Diaper Service." Sierra was sure the van was on the wrong block. None of their neighbors had a baby.

She turned to go inside when someone called from the van, "Hey, Sierra, wait up."

She whirled around and then nearly burst out laughing when she saw the delivery man jump from the front seat. Tall, handsome Drake stood before her wearing shorts and a white, short-sleeved shirt with a "Bundle of Joy" monogram above the pocket.

Chapter 8

"**W**HAT WAS GOING ON HERE WHEN I called? Is Amy still here?" Drake pulled off his sunglasses and looked past Sierra to the front porch.

"She just left. You deliver diapers?"

Drake nodded. "It's my dad's company."

"I didn't know that."

Drake gave her a sly grin. "It's not the kind of thing I go around broadcasting, you know. Now tell me what was going on with Amy."

"We were trying to plan dinner for tonight, but now it's canceled."

"Why?"

"Amy felt uncomfortable about things."

"Why?"

"Well," Sierra said, "let me ask you a question. Are you interested in going out with her?"

"No."

"She's interested in going out with you."

"So?"

"So?!"

"Yeah, so? Does that mean I'm obligated to go out with her?"

"Drake!" Sierra put her hands on her hips and shook her head. "You don't get it, do you? You hurt her feelings this morning."

"I hurt her feelings? How?"

"Because when she picked up the phone, she thought you were asking her out. Don't you see? She started to say yes, and then you told her you wanted to talk with me. She likes you, and it hurt her to find out that you were asking someone else out."

"And it's my fault Amy picked up the phone and made me think I was talking to you?"

"She didn't mean to do that. You're acting like Amy and I planned this to confuse you."

Running his fingers through his dark hair, Drake looked frustrated. "Well, it worked. I'm confused, all right."

"Oh! And you think that's our fault?"

"I'm not saying anything is anyone's fault." Drake raised his voice.

Sierra folded her arms and bit her tongue before she said something she would really regret.

"Look, Sierra, I have to go. Do you want to come with me while I make deliveries so we can talk about this?"

"I don't have any shoes on."

"So go put some shoes on."

Sierra hesitated. She wasn't sure she wanted to run

around town with Drake. Not because of the Bundle of Joy truck, but because of her concern that Amy would get upset again, the way she had about Drake coming to Sierra's house for dinner. "I don't know," she said.

"Fine!" Drake said, exasperated. "I have to go. I'll talk to you later." He hustled to the driver's side of the van, hopped in, and took off.

"Men!" Sierra muttered.

She turned to go inside when another truck rumbled up to the front of her house. Sierra threw up her arms in surrender when she saw that Randy's white truck had pulled up to the curb.

"What is going on this morning?" she muttered.

Randy slid over and rolled down the passenger window. "Hi. How's it going?"

"Don't ask!" Sierra spouted.

"Okay," Randy answered agreeably. "Let's start over again. I was on my way to my next yard job over on 52nd Street. I saw you standing out here, and I thought I'd bring you a friendly hello!" He flipped back his straight blond hair and offered her a big grin.

Sierra was not amused.

"Bad morning, huh?"

"Yes."

"Was that Drake's delivery truck?"

"Yes."

Randy cautiously ventured another question. "Is everything all set for dinner tonight?"

"No. We had to cancel the dinner."

"How come?"

"Don't ask. It's a mess."

"Is there anything I can do?" Randy asked.

"No."

Taking the hint that Sierra was not in a talkative mood, Randy smiled and said, "Well, I hope your day gets better."

"So do I."

"Oh, by the way," Randy said, "I invited Drake to go on the backpacking trip."

"You didn't! Oh, Randy!"

"What?"

Sierra grabbed her hair with both fists and giving a pull, she said, "Why do I feel as if I'm about to go totally wacko?"

Randy shrugged. "Did I do something wrong?"

"Just forget it. Now I have to call Amy and explain everything to her."

"Guess I'd better get going," Randy said sheepishly. "I'll talk to you later."

"You and everybody else," Sierra mumbled. She watched him drive away, following Amy and Drake's escape route. Then, taking the steps to the front porch two at a time, Sierra decided she needed to sit down and think things through. She retreated to the porch swing and stretched out on the soft cushions. Laying her arm across her forehead and shutting her eyes, Sierra began to sort things out.

Amy was a wreck. But maybe she was overly emotional

because of her parents, and Drake wasn't really a part of the problem after all. Any other time it wouldn't have bothered Amy that Drake called Sierra. Actually, that wasn't true. It would have bothered Amy any time. She liked the guy. But it wasn't Sierra's fault.

Drake was the problem. Why was he being so nice to Sierra and giving her all this attention? She remembered the way she felt the day before when Drake's hand had brushed the bug from her cheek. She touched the same cheek slightly, reliving the sensation. She had never felt like that before, embarrassed and warm at the same time.

I should have gone with him on his deliveries. Now he probably won't ask me out for Friday. Sierra stopped herself. *What am I thinking? Even if he did, I wouldn't go out with him! I wouldn't do that to Amy. Or Randy. Randy? Why am I worried about Randy? He wouldn't care if I went out with Drake, would he?*

The nagging voice that had been plaguing Sierra whispered to her again, *Are you sure you know what you're doing?*

She sat up and tossed her wild curls from her shoulders, hoping to shake away both the annoying whisper and her mixed-up emotions. It was no use. The confusing feelings followed her as she got up and went inside. Heading straight for the kitchen, Sierra went searching for food. Actually, she wanted sugar. For the first time she understood why Tawni used to go on sugar safaris. Chocolate is the only known cure for emotional exhaustion.

The best she could come up with were some stale miniature marshmallows and a few spoonfuls of hot fudge. Sierra warmed a bowl of fudge in the microwave and then sat down with the marshmallows and a toothpick. Her "fondue" was ready.

"Sierra!" her mother said when she entered the kitchen a few moments later. "Is that your lunch?"

"Um-hmm," Sierra answered, a gooey morsel melting in her mouth.

"Wesley said you and Amy want to have dinner here tonight."

Sierra shook her head. "It's been canceled."

"Since when?"

"Since this morning when Amy was here."

"She was here earlier?" her mom asked. "I just talked to her on the phone 10 minutes ago. I told her you were out with Drake."

Sierra dropped her marshmallow, toothpick and all, into the fudge. "You didn't."

Her mom nodded and tried one of the stale marshmallows. "When I got out of the shower, Gavin said you were out with Drake."

Chapter 9

S IERRA REALIZED HER LITTLE BROTHER MUST
have looked out the window and seen her at the
curb talking to Drake. All Sierra needed now was
for Amy to think that the minute she left, Sierra had gone
out with Drake.

Sierra ran into the study and punched in Amy's
number. "Amy, it's me. Don't hang up." Sierra sat down
in her favorite chair in the study, staring at the ceiling in
exasperation.

"I thought you were out with Drake," Amy said
accusingly.

"I was out front talking to Drake. I wasn't 'out' with
him. I was trying to explain to him that he hurt your
feelings."

"You didn't say that, did you?" Amy's voice had an
edge to it.

"Yes, I did. I wanted him to understand why it hurt you
when you realized he was trying to ask me out."

"Sierra, will you just keep your nose out of my
business?"

"What is wrong with you today? I'm on your side."

"No, you're not! Not when you go around telling Drake he hurt my feelings! That is so embarrassing. He obviously isn't interested in me. I'm not so dumb that I'm going to keep liking him."

Sierra stood up and began to pace with her hand on her forehead, stretching the phone cord around the room. "I don't get it. I was trying to stand up for you."

"I don't need you to stand up for me," Amy said coolly. "It's over."

"What's over?"

"My nonexistent relationship with Drake. He's all yours. Don't be shy. Go for it. Leave me out of your next conversation with him, and I guarantee he'll ask you out."

"How can you stop liking him so quickly?"

"A relationship takes two people," Amy said. "It was always one-sided with Drake and me. I just hoped it would change. It didn't."

"I don't know if I could go out with him, knowing that you liked him."

"Sure you could," Amy said. "In fact, I think you should."

Sierra let out a deep breath and slumped against the wall. "I don't get it. You really think I should go out with Drake?"

Amy sighed. "This whole dating thing is new to you, Sierra. Let me tell you, when a guy like Drake asks you out, you'd better say yes."

"Amy, your friendship means more to me than a date with Drake or any other guy."

"Sierra, hello! Wake up, girl! We're in high school. You're supposed to go out with guys when they ask you, not turn them down because it might hurt some other girl's feelings. Nice gesture, but I'd never expect any girl-friend to give up a potential romance for me."

"But I mean it," Sierra protested.

"I know. That's what makes you so sweet. That's why everyone, including Drake, likes you. And that's what makes it impossible for me to stay mad at you very long."

"So you're not mad anymore?"

Amy paused before saying calmly, "I'm fine with this. Really. I think you should go out with him. I'm sure he'll ask you again."

Sierra wished she could see Amy's face so she would know without a doubt that Amy was being honest.

That evening Sierra still felt uneasy about Amy's blessing and decided she would join Wes on a walk to Mount Tabor Park with Brutus. Maybe it was time to take Wes up on his offer to play big brother. He'd probably enjoy the opportunity to pour out his wisdom for her.

They put the leash on Brutus and were rounding the side of the house when Drake walked up the front steps.

"Hey, Drake," Wes called out. "Over here."

Sierra felt her heart pounding.

"How's it going?" Wes asked.

"Pretty good. You guys heading out for a walk?"

Wes glanced at Sierra and then said, "Sierra was looking for some company. You want to fill in for me, Drake?"

"Sure." Drake looked as if he had just stepped out of

the shower with his thick, dark hair slicked back. The blue T-shirt and jeans were a contrast to the bright-white Bundle of Joy uniform he had worn that morning.

Wes handed the leash to Sierra and said, "Make sure you have the big lug back by midnight."

"Which one?" Sierra muttered.

"I heard that," Drake said. "Which way are we going?" He reached over and roughed up Brutus's furry mane.

"Left, if you want to go to the park."

"Fine with me."

Brutus let out an impatient woof and took off. Sierra pulled on the leash. "The other way, Brutus. Go left."

"He actually knows his right from his left?" Drake asked.

"No, but we're working on it."

They walked a block and a half in awkward silence before Drake said, "Can I tell you my side about Amy?"

"Sure."

"I don't know what Amy has told you, but this is how I see it. A bunch of us went to the Blazers game. Maybe you remember—we were planning it during lunch one day at school. Amy sort of asked for a ride, and when I agreed, it was as if we were going out. I saw it as giving a friend a ride. I don't know what she considered it to be."

Amy had been so excited. Sierra recalled teasing her about how she had manipulated Drake into asking her out. Amy had also set up the dinner plans to encourage Drake's interest.

Apparently, Drake had never felt the same about Amy.

Amy had been the instigator all along.

"I can understand your trying to defend Amy," Drake said. "But I'm not sure it was fair for you to make me out to be the bad guy."

"Maybe I jumped to conclusions," Sierra admitted.

"Jumped?" Drake echoed. "How about catapulted?"

Sierra laughed. "Okay, so I catapulted. All I know is that it hurt Amy's feelings when she answered the phone, and you were calling for me, not her."

"Whoa, wait a minute," Drake said. "I didn't know Amy was at your house this morning, and I sure didn't know she was the one on the phone. Are you telling me I don't have the right to ask a girl out if I know someone else is interested in me?"

Sierra saw his point. Still, Amy was her friend. Her good friend, which was something she didn't have an abundance of at the moment.

Drake continued. "What if I don't want to go out with her? Aren't I free to make my own decisions? Or do I have to sit home, just so I won't potentially hurt her feelings?"

They came to a busy cross street, and Brutus lurched forward, galloping off the curb.

"Wait, there's a car coming!" Sierra yelled. She jerked on the leash and suddenly felt Drake's warm hand on top of hers.

"Here, I'll take him," Drake offered. He grabbed the leash and spoke firmly to Brutus. "Come on, boy. Hold up a minute."

If Sierra's heart had been racing before, it was sprinting

now. She saw Drake in a new light. He was right. It wasn't fair for her to judge him only on Amy's view of what her relationship with Drake should be. Drake had a say in things, too.

"Look, I want to be straight with you, Sierra. I don't date a lot. I made it a point last year to hang out with a lot of different people and not to go out with just one person."

Sierra knew that was true. Drake was friends with everyone and had even been called a flirt because he didn't go out with the same girl twice.

"I've been thinking about this a lot. Would you like to go out with me?"

"You mean to the movies on Friday?"

"Yes, but more than that," Drake said. "I mean date. You know, be together this summer. I'd really like to spend time with you and get to know you better."

Sierra noticed that Drake's forehead was beginning to perspire. His voice sounded calm and confident, but she knew he must be feeling as nervous as she was.

Well . . . he was right about Amy. And he is an incredible guy. Sierra thought.

"Okay," she said.

Boy, did that sound lame! Sierra chided herself. *Couldn't you get a little more enthusiastic here? Drake just asked you out!*

Then, before Sierra could stop herself, she blurted out, "Why me?"

Chapter 10

"WHY YOU?" DRAKE LAUGHED.

"What I mean is, you can have any girl you want. Why in the world do you want to go out with me?"

Drake scratched the back of his neck. "I don't know. Do I have to have a reason? Isn't it enough that I like you and want to spend time with you?"

Sierra edged a little closer to Drake as they entered the park and turned up a tree-lined path. "I guess so. I'm flattered, that's all. I love this park, don't you? All the trees make it feel so secluded. Like a secret hiding place."

"It's nice," Drake agreed.

The trail wound upward, and they stopped talking and starting huffing with each rapid step. Drake's long stride proved to be a challenge for Sierra to keep up with. They didn't talk again until they reached the top of the hill where a spectacular view of the city stretched out below them. The bright summer sun hung low in the west, lacing the long row of scalloped clouds with a satin ribbon of peach.

"It's beautiful," Sierra murmured.

Drake casually slipped his arm around her shoulder, holding Brutus's leash tightly with his right hand. "Beautiful," Drake repeated.

This is so wonderful! Sierra thought. *I love feeling his arm around me. I wonder if he's going to kiss me. Wait, what am I thinking? Why would he kiss me? We hardly know each other.*

It was the first time Sierra had been overwhelmed with such strong feelings about a guy. Everything was coming at her so fast. She both liked the emotional rush and felt threatened by it. It was like the feeling she had on the Tilt-O-Wheel ride at the county fair when she was a kid. She loved the sensation of the gravity taking over, but felt anxious at the same time because she was no longer in control.

Something stronger than she was at work. With the rush of emotion came the fear of doing something she would later regret. On the Tilt-O-Wheel, she'd feared throwing up in public when she got off the ride. But with Drake, she didn't know exactly what it was she feared. Some kind of warning system was going off in her head, though.

"We'd better head back," Sierra heard herself say. "This guy's going to need a drink of water."

"I saw a fountain back there," Drake said. "Can he drink from there?"

"Sure."

They turned to go. Drake kept his arm around her

shoulders. He seemed to think the gesture was completely normal. She hoped he couldn't feel her blood pumping at top speed through her shoulders, making her feel warmer than usual in her shorts and T-shirt on this mild summer's evening.

Drake led Brutus to the fountain and dropped his arm from Sierra's shoulders while he let Brutus lap up the cool water. She immediately missed the warmth and security Drake's arm had given her.

When Brutus had had enough, he led Sierra and Drake to a bench beside a blooming rose garden, where he lay down.

"Looks like Brutus wants a rest before going home," Drake said. "Not a bad idea."

He sat down on the bench, and Sierra sat next to him. Not too close, not too far away.

The summer sky was still lit by the pastels that streamed across the evening clouds. It would be light for at least another half an hour. The park was alive with people biking along the trails, playing on the swings, and finishing up their barbecue picnics. Sierra felt content.

"I'm glad we straightened things out," Sierra said. She felt like telling Drake that Amy had given Sierra her blessing to date him. But then she thought if she brought Amy's name up, she might say things the wrong way, and Amy would get mad at her all over again.

"Yeah, well, I knew you'd see the light," he teased. Drake had a way of jutting out his chin when he was after something he wanted. Sierra had noticed that before when he had begged cookies from her at school. Right now his chin was sticking out, firm and determined.

This guy knows what he wants and goes after it. I still can't believe I'm the one he wants to be with! I love the way he's strong and so good-looking, and yet he's not too proud to drive a diaper delivery truck around town. This guy is perfect for me.

"It's going to be a great summer," Drake murmured, slipping his arm around her shoulders again.

Sierra slid just a tiny bit closer. "That's what my mom keeps promising me. But the way things were going this morning, I wasn't so sure I'd make it through the day, let alone the whole summer!"

"Oh, I think you'll make it," Drake said, smiling.

With energetic bursts, Sierra's mind flashed images of what the summer was going to be like. Drake hiking with her on the backpacking trip. Drake taking her out to dinner. Drake buying her popcorn at the movies. Drake sitting with his arm around her on the porch swing. Drake giving her, her very first kiss.

Chapter 11

T WAS NEARLY **1:00** IN THE MORNING, AND Sierra tossed and turned in her bed. She couldn't sleep. The whole evening with Drake had fueled her emotions. In the stillness of her room, she relit each feeling and let it burn itself out.

They had walked home from the park hand in hand. Her parents were sitting in the porch swing when they arrived. After putting Brutus in the backyard, Sierra and Drake had sat on the porch talking with her mom and dad. Then Drake scored extra points by asking Sierra's dad if it would be okay with him if Drake took Sierra to the movies Friday night.

Mr. Jensen said yes, and Mrs. Jensen wore a subtle, pleased smile. When Drake left, they all waved good-bye from the front porch.

No kiss. But then Sierra didn't want him to kiss her just like that the first night. The whole summer stretched before them.

She had gone to bed right after that and had stared at the ceiling and kicked at the sheets for more than three hours now. Her mind refused to shift into a lower gear.

Part of her nervous energy was directed toward Amy. What would she say to Amy tomorrow? Would it really be okay with her if Sierra started going out with Drake? What would it be like for Amy and Drake to both be at the back-packers' meeting? Should she warn Amy ahead of time so it wouldn't be awkward for her to see Drake there?

And would Randy still feel comfortable coming around now that Drake was going to be a permanent part of her summer schedule? A smile curled Sierra's lips in the dark, silent bedroom as she thought of the contrast between Randy and Drake. Drake's hands weren't rough like Randy's, and they didn't smell like cut grass. Tawni would certainly be surprised when she found out she and Drake were a couple. Sierra glanced over at the vacant bed. If only Tawni were here now, then Sierra would have someone to wake up to listen to all of Sierra's plans for the summer.

Sierra never would have dreamed this day would have turned out the way it did. It had moved from Amy's crying in the kitchen that morning to Sierra's watching the sunset with Drake. Sierra smiled. This was a day to remember.

Feeling content with that thought, Sierra finally fell asleep.

The next morning, Sierra dressed extra carefully because she felt so special. She pulled back her hair in a loose ponytail and picked out her newest—and sub-sequently favorite—pair of dangly earrings. Her usual summer wardrobe of shorts and a T-shirt seemed blah today. She rooted through the back of her closet, searching for something that would make her look as lighthearted as she felt. Then she saw it—the long gauze dress that Tawni called her "granny gown."

Sierra slipped it over her head and smiled at the thought that Tawni wasn't here to make any of her rude comments about the way Sierra dressed. She was a free spirit and had insisted to Tawni for years that her clothes expressed her art of living. Her sister would smirk and say, "They're an expression all right."

She placed a silver dove necklace on a long black ribbon around her neck, finishing off the outfit. Sierra looked in the oval mirror above her antique dresser and smiled approvingly. Drake's interest in her had given her much confidence. It felt good to be admired, to be wanted. Sierra couldn't remember the last time she had felt this way. It was terrific.

And no one could change her sunny outlook at work. She wore a permanent smile as she served cinnamon rolls and filled yogurt cones. And she was still grinning that evening as she helped her mother do the dishes before rushing off to the youth group meeting at church.

Since Sierra's family had moved to Portland, they had visited a number of churches. They attended one across the bridge in Washington for a while because Tawni was interested in their college group. But the church they ended up at was only a few miles from their house and also happened to be the church in which Randy grew up. His parents and Sierra's were in the same home Bible study group. Amy started going with Sierra since her family didn't have a church they attended regularly. Sierra wasn't sure of Drake's church background.

Sierra arrived early and glanced around the parking lot, looking for Drake's car. It wasn't there yet. Neither was Amy's Volvo. Randy's truck was in one of the first parking spots; he usually came early. Sierra wondered if Drake had come with him. She entered the youth room and scanned the group, looking for Drake.

Randy spotted her and waved from the corner. For several weeks, he had been trying to organize a band, and it looked as if they finally had everything in place. Tre, a guy from school, stood in the center of the group, tuning up his guitar. Randy adjusted one of the speakers, and a few minutes later the room was filled with live music.

They sounded great, but Sierra was distracted. She nervously watched the door for Drake or Amy. As she waited, she practiced what she was going to say to Amy. But Amy never showed up.

Drake came in a few minutes late and stuck close to Sierra. She was proud to be with him, being keenly aware of the looks some of the other girls were giving her and the way they watched Drake.

"Do you want to sit down?" Drake asked Sierra after she had introduced him to all her friends.

They settled down near the front just as Shane, the youth leader, called everyone to find a seat. Of medium height and muscular, Shane had a commanding voice and boundless energy.

"Hey, you guys! We're glad you're here," Shane boomed to the crowd. "Let's get going."

For the first 20 minutes, they sang, accompanied by Randy's band. The room seemed much fuller than it had in weeks past. The band helped to boost attendance, Sierra was sure, and it added to the liveliness of the songs.

"Short-term pleasure, long-term pain," Shane said as everyone sat down after the last song. "That's our topic tonight. Short-term pleasure, long-term pain. I want you to form small groups and discuss what that means to you."

Sierra turned to Drake, and he said, "It means what it says. Some things you do are enjoyable for the moment, but they produce painful results."

"Like eating chocolate," said Jana, the girl on the other side of Drake, who had welcomed herself into their little group. "Chocolate makes me happy while I'm eating it, but it doesn't do my body any good in the long run." Jana wore her blond hair cut short above her ears. She had a wide smile and a button nose. She was thick around the middle and shorter than Sierra.

"Any examples?" Shane asked after a few minutes, looking around the room. "How about this group here?" He motioned toward Sierra.

"Chocolate," Jana called out.

"Okay, good answer. Chocolate can be a short-term pleasure that can produce long-term pain. Good. Next group?"

As Shane collected more answers, Sierra thought about Amy.

I should have called her instead of waiting and assuming she would show up, she chided herself. *I should have called her just to let her know Drake would be here—kind of with me. Well, hopefully she'll be at the meeting afterward, and I can try to explain things to her then.*

"Okay," Shane said, pulling everyone's attention back to the front, "let's look at a verse I believe will help all of us. If you have your Bible with you, I suggest you underline this one. And if you didn't bring your Bible, bring it next week, okay? Anyone who doesn't have a Bible, let me know, and we'll get you one."

A rustling noise filled the room as people reached for their Bibles. Sierra felt bad. She had forgotten hers, and that wasn't like her. But tonight she had been so preoccupied that she had run out the door without it. She would listen closely, though, and remember the verse Shane read. That way when she got home, she could mark it in her Bible.

Actually, quite a few days had passed since she had spent time reading her Bible or praying. It was easy to rationalize that lapse, because with the beginning of summer, her schedule had changed and her life had become hectic. Sierra knew she needed that regular time talking to God and listening to Him to stay on track. She silently promised herself and God that she would read extra chapters tonight.

"Got your Bibles ready? Here's the verse: Hebrews

12:11. It says, 'All discipline for the moment seems not to be joyful, but sorrowful; yet to those who have been trained by it, afterwards it yields the peaceful fruit of righteousness.' "

For the next 10 minutes, Shane talked about what discipline meant and how Christians needed to be trained in discipline to have peace with themselves and with God.

Sierra tried hard to listen, but she kept wondering if Drake was going to reach for her hand or slip his arm around her while Shane talked. She wasn't sure whether she wanted Drake's attention. Unfortunately, all the anticipation and subsequent disappointment kept her from hearing Shane's message. Sierra did remember the Scripture reference, though, and she planned to mark it in her Bible when she got home.

After Shane closed the meeting in prayer, Randy and the band played again. Then all the people going on the backpacking trip went into another room to meet. Amy didn't show up, which worried Sierra.

Shane handed out a list of everything they needed to bring, along with a permission slip that had to be filled out by their parents before they left Monday morning. Ten minutes into the meeting, Wesley walked into the room.

Shane looked up with obvious relief. "Good. Wes is here. You guys, this is our other trip leader, Wes Jensen. He's our wilderness expert. Any questions, you can ask him."

Sierra gave Wes a look that reflected her surprise. He

winked in return and started asking if everyone had proper hiking boots.

Sierra smiled ruefully. With Wes as a leader, Drake as her new boyfriend, and the tension she was experiencing with Randy and Amy, this was going to be some trip!

Chapter 12

A S SOON AS SIERRA GOT HOME, SHE PHONED Amy. But Amy's answering machine picked up the call. Sierra tried again the next morning and got the machine a second time. Finally, exasperated, she drove over to Amy's house, and Amy answered the door.

"I called," Sierra said. "Why didn't you pick up the phone?"

"I was in the shower." Amy sounded defensive.

She led Sierra to her bedroom. On the wall behind Amy's bed hung a gorgeous old quilt stitched together from patchwork squares by Amy's grandma. The bed wasn't made, and belongings were scattered around the room—a clump of dirty clothes on the floor by the closet, a pile of papers on the desk, a stack of magazines by the bed with a half-empty glass of milk on top.

Sierra sat in the chair by Amy's desk and began to chat as if there were no reason for things to be strained between them.

"You're still going backpacking, aren't you? I missed

you at the meeting last night."

"I had to fill in for a girl at work who called in sick. I don't know if I'm going backpacking after all." Amy avoided Sierra's eyes.

"Why not? We've been planning this for a long time. You already asked for time off from work, didn't you? I brought you a permission slip. It needs to be filled out by your parents before we leave Monday."

"I heard Drake is going." Amy arched her eyebrows, waiting for Sierra's response.

"Yes, he is. I've been trying to find the best way to tell you what's happening."

"Did he ask you out?" Amy asked.

"Yes. Tonight."

"So you're going out with him! Are you excited about it?" Amy looked as if she were happy for Sierra.

"Yes."

"That's great, Sierra." Amy smiled and adjusted some books stacked on her nightstand.

"Do you really mean that? You're not upset about this?"

"No. I told you. This is high school. You're supposed to go out with guys when they ask you. Or at least the ones worth going out with."

"Thanks for understanding," Sierra said, relieved. "I didn't want things to be strained between us now that Drake is going backpacking, too. Oh, and did I tell you? Wes is also coming."

Amy looked up. "He is?"

"Yes. Shane asked him to come along as an assistant.

You didn't have anything to do with that, did you?"

Amy shrugged her shoulders. "I just suggested it a couple of times. You know that."

Sierra lowered her voice. "How are things with your parents?"

"They seem fine. As if nothing happened. I'm waiting for them to blow up again, you know?"

Sierra didn't know. Her parents didn't have that kind of relationship, so she couldn't understand what it was like to have to tiptoe around your own home, trying not to irritate someone who was already upset.

"I really appreciate your understanding about Drake. He's a great guy. Thanks for being so nice about everything."

Amy looked down. "Don't thank me. You're the one who attracted him. He was never interested in me. I was fooling myself to think he could ever like me. Anyway, it seems pretty clear you two are getting along great."

"God will have someone special for you, Amy. Just wait and see." Sierra couldn't believe she was saying those words. Over the years, she had heard other people using that line, and she hated it. Why did it seem natural to say it now? What was happening to her?

"I have to do some things this morning before I go to work," Sierra said, changing the subject. "I'm working till nine tonight. New hours Mrs. Kraus is trying out. Come see me if you can."

"I'm working from five to nine," Amy said. "And all day tomorrow."

"Then I guess I'll see you at church on Sunday."

Amy smiled as Sierra left and said, "Have a good time with Drake."

"I will. Thanks."

Sierra hopped into her car and drove downtown to the Outback Store to get her supplies for the backpacking trip. She wished she could feel settled about Amy, but a thread of tension still hung between them. Amy seemed to be holding something back. Or was she only imagining it?

Next door to the Outback Store was a pharmacy. Sierra decided she needed to buy some items there first, things she had never bought before. The biodegradable soap could wait. She wanted to buy some makeup.

That night, after a quick shower, Sierra slipped into her favorite jeans shorts and white cotton shirt. With bracelets, necklace, and earrings in place, she started to work on trying to tame her hair.

This is pointless, Sierra thought after a while. No matter what she did, her hair cascaded in unruly curls from the crown of her head down to the middle of her back. For years, other girls had admired Sierra's locks and said they would trade hair with her any day. She would have been only too glad to accommodate them.

Sierra wasn't so concerned about her hair tonight. She was too excited about the small bag of cosmetics she had bought at the pharmacy. This was an adventure for Sierra. The only times she had worn makeup were the scattered occasions when Tawni had imposed her cosmetic skills on her.

Tonight, though, she was on her own. Twirling the mascara wand the way she remembered Tawni doing it, Sierra started from the outside lashes and worked her way toward the inside lashes. Leaning toward the bathroom mirror with her mouth open in an *O,* Sierra made each stroke with slow, deliberate care. Stepping back and blinking slightly, she felt pleased. Her eyes did look bigger, just as Tawni had said. She finished with a little brown eyeliner the way Tawni applied it—thin and even, then softened with a Q-Tip. So far so good.

For lipstick, Sierra had bought a gloss with a natural red shade. She liked it immediately, not only for the way it highlighted her lips, but also for the way it smelled like fresh strawberries.

I wonder if Drake will notice.

Sierra felt herself blush slightly as she pictured Drake kissing her tonight. She stuck the tube of strawberry lip gloss in her pocket and gave herself a final look.

Ready or not, Drake, here I come!

Chapter 13

*I*T WAS A GOOD THING DRAKE SHOWED UP ON time. If Sierra had tried to contain her butterflies any longer, they would have started to escape out her ears.

"You look great," he said when she greeted him at the front door.

After a few last-minute reminders from Sierra's parents, she and Drake were on their way.

Instead of Drake's old, beat-up car, an expensive-looking blue sedan sat at the curb.

"It's my mom's car," he explained as he opened the passenger door. Sierra slid onto the clean upholstery. "I told her I wanted tonight to be special, and she said I could use it."

"That was nice of her," Sierra said.

"She's a nice mom," Drake agreed, getting in and fastening his seat belt. "Sure beats the delivery van."

Sierra laughed. "I'm glad you didn't pick me up in that!"

Before Drake started the engine, he reached over and

took Sierra's hand in his. In the shelter of his large, cool hand, Sierra realized how clammy hers had become. Hopefully, he wouldn't notice.

"How're you doing?" Drake smiled at her.

"Great!" Sierra said. She was startled to hear her voice squeak out. She cleared her throat. "Well, maybe a little nervous. It was kind of a full day."

Drake gave her hand a squeeze, then let go and turned the key in the ignition.

Sierra tried to organize all of her thoughts, which were flying around in her head like popcorn kernels: her feelings about herself, her looks, her outfit, her posture.

Should she try to sit closer to him? Was that last squirt of "Vanilla Earth Scents" too much? Should she roll down the window? Would it be tacky to pull down the visor mirror and make sure her mascara hadn't smeared?

"My day was pretty full, too," Drake said. "Three new accounts in the Powell district and none of the delivery bags were loaded in the van. I had to go back twice because I thought they were all newborn, but one was the 12-to-18-month size."

Sierra started to laugh.

Drake glanced at her, and then realized how trivial his stress sounded to her. "Yes, siree," he said with a tease in his voice, "haulin' diapers around town is a mighty tough job."

"But somebody's gotta do it, right?" Sierra said.

"It's probably not quite as stressful as getting the swirl-e-que just right on the top of those yogurt cones, is it?"

Sierra laughed again and started to relax. "You have no idea. And then there's the mixed factor. Some customers want the chocolate and vanilla swirled and others want only chocolate or only vanilla. I tell you, it's completely exhausting."

Drake smiled. He liked her, she could tell.

"I bought the tickets before coming to your house," Drake said. "I wanted to make sure they weren't sold out."

They parked at the theater and walked inside, still teasing each other about their hard day's work. His six-foot-two frame towered above her as they stood in line for popcorn. She loved being so much shorter than Drake. It made her feel dainty. Randy was only a few inches taller than Sierra, and when she held hands with him, she felt more like his twin.

Drake led her to a center aisle in the theater, and with their tub of popcorn and two large soft drinks, they maneuvered past four other people. Settling in, Sierra felt her crazy emotions calm down. They balanced the popcorn between them and began to munch away. The movie started. Sierra wondered if Drake was going to hold her hand. It would be difficult since she kept using that hand to scoop up the popcorn.

Sierra began to eat faster. The sooner the popcorn was gone, the sooner their hands would be empty. Drake seemed to be in no hurry and ate only a small handful every five minutes or so. Feeling like a pig, Sierra settled back, slowly munching the popcorn at the same pace as Drake, and enjoyed the movie.

"How did you like it?" Drake asked as they left the theater.

"Lots of action!" Sierra said, looking up at his clean-shaven face in the light of the lobby. "It was good. I can't remember what other show I saw that actress in, but I liked her in this role a lot better."

"You hungry?"

Sierra folded her hands across her stomach. "Are you kidding? After all that popcorn?"

"Something to drink maybe?"

"I'm with you. Wherever you want to go is fine with me."

Drake slipped his arm around her shoulder, and Sierra wrapped her arm around his waist. No one could have described to her how good it felt. She suddenly understood lyrics to love songs, comments from girlfriends, underlying themes from romance movies. There was no feeling like this in the world.

Drake drove to the Brewed Awakenings coffee shop, and they sat at a table outside. He had hot chocolate; she sipped tea. They talked about their families, their plans for college, their favorite cartoon characters, and what the lyrics meant to a song that played in the background.

Sierra liked the way Drake looked directly at her when she spoke, as if drinking in her words. Never before in her life had she felt as special and sought after as she did tonight.

Drake drove her home, laughing over a joke she told him. He pulled up in front of the house and turned off the engine. Sierra felt her heart racing. She wanted to reach for the strawberry lip gloss in her pocket but decided that that would be too obvious. She undid her seat belt. Drake undid his. He shifted in his seat. She shifted in hers. Certainly, he would notice in the glow from the streetlight how rosy her cheeks were turning.

"Sierra," he said tenderly, reaching for her hand.

She linked her fingers with his, hoping her wildly pounding heart would calm down.

"Before you go, I want to ask you something."

This is it! Sierra thought excitedly. *Drake is such a gentleman, he's even going to ask me before he kisses me, the way he asked Dad if he could take me out.*

With a slight smile, Sierra invited his question. "Yes?"

"I don't do this with every girl I go out with," Drake said. His slicked-back hair had fallen forward on the right side, giving him a vulnerable, schoolboy look. "But you're different, and if you don't mind . . ."

He squeezed her hand a little tighter. Sierra held her breath.

"Yes?"

"Will you pray with me?"

Chapter 14

*S*IERRA SLOWLY BEGAN TO BREATHE AGAIN. A BIG lump refused to go down her throat.

"Sure," she said, closing her eyes, swallowing hard, and licking her strawberry-less lips.

His words were brief but seemed heartfelt, as Drake thanked God for their time together and asked for His direction for each of their futures. By the time he said, "Amen," Sierra had come down from her cloud.

"Thanks," she said. "I had a wonderful time."

"So did I," he replied. "Let me get your door."

Sierra remembered what Amy had said about Drake opening the door for her. She didn't remember Amy mentioning anything about praying with him, though. They walked to the front door, and before Sierra could let her exhausted imagination come up with all the possible scenarios of what might happen next, Drake smiled at her and said, "Good night." Then he turned and hustled to the car as if he were on a tight curfew to get home.

Sierra felt drained. Happy and sad at the same time. Delighted and frustrated. She opened the door and heard the TV in the family room.

"Sierra?" her mom called out. "Did you have a good time?"

"Yes, it was wonderful. I'm going to bed." She headed upstairs, still lost in a daze. It wasn't that she didn't want to pray with Drake. She thought that was great. It made her realize, though, how long it had been since she had had a good, long conversation with God. What had happened? What had crowded her time so much?

Ten minutes later, as Sierra climbed into bed, her mother tapped on her door. "How did everything go?"

"It was totally wonderful. He laughed at my jokes, opened my door, bought me popcorn, and prayed with me. I think I'm in love."

Mrs. Jensen laughed. "Are you serious?"

"Actually, I don't know what I feel. He held my hand and prayed with me. I liked that. A lot. It was just different from what I expected."

"What did you expect?" her mom asked, stretching out on Tawni's bed.

Sierra felt embarrassed telling her mom, but they had always been honest about everything. "Well, I guess I thought he might kiss me."

"And he didn't?"

"No."

"What would his kiss have meant to you?"

"Meant to me? I don't know. That he liked me. That he wanted to go out with me again. That he thought I was attractive."

Her mom propped herself up on her elbow and rested her head in her hand. "You don't think he felt those things without kissing you?"

Sierra thought hard. "He made me feel all those things. I guess I just expected a kiss. I don't know. My emotions were running around in my head all night like escaped zoo animals!"

Mrs. Jensen laughed. "Sounds normal to me. And Drake sounds better than normal. I'm glad he didn't kiss you."

"Why?"

"It's better for your first kiss, or any kiss for that matter, to be given only after you know what you're giving away."

Sierra was silent.

"Good night, honey. I'm glad you had such a good time." She got up to leave. "Oh, Amy stopped by tonight. She had some questions for Wes about her backpack. He helped her get set up for the trip. Are you almost ready?"

"I think so. Mom? Have you noticed that Amy finds reasons to be around Wes? I'm sure she has a crush on him."

"Yes," was all her mother said as she stood by the open door.

"Don't you think it's ridiculous? Wes would never like her back the same way. She's only setting herself up to be hurt."

"Have you told her that?"

"Not yet."

"Then don't," her mom said and exited, closing the door behind her.

Sierra snapped off her light and shook her head in the darkened room. How could her own mother say that? Then she smiled. She couldn't wait to replay the entire night in her mind, reliving each feeling, as she had Wednesday night after their walk to Mount Tabor. Then she remembered she'd planned to spend some time praying tonight. And yesterday she'd planned to mark that verse from Hebrews in her Bible. But she felt so tired. It was as if her emotions, which had been running wild all night, were finally tucked away in their cages, safe and sound.

As Sierra closed her mascara-brushed lashes, she fell fast asleep.

Chapter 15

MONDAY MORNING SIERRA AND WES WERE the first to arrive at the church parking lot wearing their camping gear and sporting their full backpacks.

"Wes," Sierra said, deciding to take advantage of the few moments they had alone, "I've been meaning to talk with you about something. You said last week that if I had anything I wanted to talk about, I could come to you."

Wesley looked interested. "Guy problems?"

"No. I wanted to warn you about possible girl troubles."

"Excuse me?"

Randy's white truck pulled into the parking lot and roared past Sierra and Wes. The three backpacks in the truck bed slid forward as Randy came to a halt. They could hear laughter from inside the cab as he turned off the engine. Randy opened one door while Drake opened the other and got out. Amy rolled out behind Drake, laughing the hardest of them all.

A lump formed in Sierra's throat. "I'll talk to you later," she mumbled to Wes.

"If you're going to tell me what I think you are, don't bother. I'm not that naive, Sierra Mae." Wes rolled his eyes.

"Hi!" Drake called out. A donut was wedged between his front teeth like a dog bone.

Amy had powdered sugar all over her hair and a blob of jelly on her nose. She was still laughing as she approached Wes and Sierra.

"Don't ever agree to ride with those two," she warned. "Especially if they're armed with food."

The lump in Sierra's throat swelled. Who put the jelly on her nose? Randy? Was he suddenly interested in Amy now that Sierra and Drake were together? Or was it Drake? Was Amy flirting with Drake and was he flirting back? A dark cloud of horrible thoughts crossed Sierra's mind.

I think I want to go home, she thought.

"Donut?" Randy held out the open box to Sierra.

"No thanks." She sat down on the grass next to her backpack. Drake came over and put his backpack down next to hers.

"Sure you don't want one?" Drake asked. "They're fresh as a winter snowfall." With that he demonstrated the powdered sugar sprinkling from his donut, which accounted for Amy's dandruff outbreak.

"Here, Sierra," Randy said. "Sniff this jelly donut and tell me what it smells like to you."

He had a gleam of mischief in his eye.

"Don't do it!" Amy warned. "If you smell it, he'll

smash it into your face." She wiped the jelly off her nose with her finger and bent down to clean it on the grass.

Sierra tried hard to smile and enter into their banter. But it was their joke. The three of them were having fun together. Sierra hadn't been a part of it. Why did that bother her so much? All four of them had goofed around in the lunchroom during the school year; yet somehow this felt different. As if she and Drake should be the ones sharing personal jokes, not him playing tricks on Amy.

Shane arrived with a car full of backpackers. Two other cars pulled into the parking lot at the same time. After nearly an hour of organizing, everyone talking at once, and finally a group prayer, they loaded up in the church van and took off.

Randy and Drake were the first to clamber into the van, and they headed to the back bench seat. Sierra made sure she was the next one in and planted herself beside Drake. It bothered her that he didn't seem to wait for her; nor did it seem that he planned to save a seat for her next to him. What was going on?

"Do you mind changing spots with me?" Drake asked before they took off. "There's a little more leg room on the end."

Sierra obliged and scooted over between Randy and Drake while he slid past her and stretched out his legs in the narrow aisle.

Now this is really strange, sitting between Randy and Drake, she thought. *A week ago I would have been sitting next to Randy, probably holding his hand or sleeping on his shoulder. Now I'm with Drake, so is he going to put his arm around me? How will that feel with Randy sitting right there? Oh, why is my head pounding?*

As the van moved north on the freeway, Sierra momentarily solved her problems by folding her arms across her middle and sliding down in the seat. With her eyes closed, she pretended to be asleep as she tried to figure everything out.

She could hear Amy's voice carrying from the front where she sat behind Wes, who was in the front passenger seat. She peppered him with questions about backpacking technique—questions like, "How tightly should I adjust the straps? Will my back hurt? Should the pack ride on my hips or at my waist?"

Unlike Sierra, Amy definitely had hips for her pack to ride on. She also had a tiny waist, which was emphasized today by her choice of hiking apparel. The shorts weren't exactly durable fabric, and when she reached up, her clean white T-shirt rose just enough to show her belly button. Definitely not a practical choice for the day.

Sierra had been backpacking many times before and she knew what worked best. That's why she wore rugged, six-pocket, green army shorts and a dark-green T-shirt covered with one of her dad's old flannel shirts. Now that was practical.

So why did she feel like such a slob? And why was Drake ignoring her and talking to Jana in the seat in front of them? Jana had a pocket-sized game of Connect Four, and she and Drake played it all the way to the hiking trail.

Every time Sierra peeked at Randy, he was looking out the window and appeared to be lost in thought. As the van sped toward Mount Adams, Sierra let her own thoughts unwind like a long roll of paper towels. And like a roll of printed paper towels, the same pattern kept repeating itself in Sierra's mind. Not long rows of blue geese with pink ribbons on their necks, but long, connecting thoughts on how she felt about Drake and what he felt about her. The pattern of Randy and where his friendship fit in all this also ran through her mind. And every time Amy giggled, Sierra wondered if she had made such a terrific choice in a best friend after all.

The more Sierra listened to Drake and Jana play their game, the more she felt left out. *I should do something to make Drake pay attention to me. No, it's better this way,* she decided. *It's like we're together, but we're still friends with everyone else. I should talk to Randy then. But what if he thinks I'm trying to flirt with him? Randy doesn't know that Drake and I are together now, does he? What if he tries to hold my hand? Would he do that? Why isn't Drake holding my hand?*

"Ha!" Drake's voice cut through her thoughts. "I did it. Right there. I connected four."

Sierra wished she could find a way to connect four of her unsettled thoughts—especially before this back-packing group hit the trail. She knew what it was like to enjoy the beauty of God's world in the back country and, at the same time, feel as if even God's creation has turned against you. Hiking was not a time for resolving unsettled relationships. It was a time for everyone to work together as a team. The last thing Sierra felt was that she was part of a team.

Chapter 16

"TURN HERE," WES TOLD SHANE. "THE MAP says to park in the area by the Pacific Crest Trail. That's down this road."

The van bumped over the dirt road, and everyone joked and made noise as if they were on a ride at Disneyland.

"Over there," Wes directed. "It's on the north side. Keep going."

"This road is ridiculous!" Shane said as they hit another big bump.

Sierra looked out Randy's window at the mountain looming before them. "Is that the one that erupted?"

Randy turned to her. "No. This is Mount Adams. Mount Saint Helens is the one that blew her stack. I've been there a bunch of times with my dad because he's worked on different geology teams, but I've never been here."

"I didn't know your dad was a geologist," Drake said, leaning close to Sierra and looking out Randy's window. "Are you the experienced nature boy when it comes to living in the wild?"

"Something like that," Randy said, his lopsided smile appearing for the first time since the trip began.

"What about you, Sierra?" Drake asked. "Didn't you grow up near Lake Tahoe?"

Sierra nodded and leaned back, aware of how near he was to her and how equally close she was to Randy. They hit another bump, and her head banged against Drake's shoulder.

"Oops, sorry," she mumbled.

Drake slipped his arm around her shoulders as if he were her human seat belt. "Go ahead. What were you going to say?"

"I don't remember," Sierra said, realizing their relationship had now been revealed.

She glanced over at Randy. He turned his head and looked out the window.

"Did your family do a lot of camping and backpacking while you were growing up?" Drake asked her.

"Yes, but Wes is more of a pro than I am. So is Randy." She hoped Randy would turn to them and come back into the conversation. He didn't.

"I'm sticking with you guys," Drake said, giving Sierra's arm a little squeeze. "You want to hear a confession? This is my first backpacking trip."

"I'm sure you'll like it," Sierra said.

"I've only been camping once. My dad's idea of roughing it is staying at a hotel that doesn't have cable," Drake joked.

Sierra laughed. Randy didn't.

The van came to an abrupt halt.

"This is the place," Shane said. "Now, I want everyone to help unpack the trailer."

They filed out, and their laughter tumbled out of the van with them. Sierra pitched in and hoisted packs out of the trailer. Many of the girls were giggling and standing around, admitting they weren't sure how to put on their packs and asking the guys to help them.

"Don't look at me," Drake said to Jana. "I'm the novice here. Ask Sierra. She's our nature woman."

"What do I do with this strap, Nature Woman?" Jana asked.

"That's for you to hang a water bottle or canteen on. Did you bring one?"

"No." Jana looked embarrassed.

"It was on the list," Sierra said.

"I know, but we didn't have one at home."

"I brought extra water bottles," Shane said, stepping into their conversation. "Who needs one?"

Five people responded, "I do."

Sierra caught her brother's glance, and she could tell he felt the same way she did about this trip. Shane hadn't said if he had done much backpacking, but he clearly was glad when Wes agreed to come along. Sierra was glad Wes was there, too. She had looked at the maps Wes was given the night before and was relieved to see it was an easy hike. Only 12 miles total and a gain of less than 2,000 feet in elevation.

The elevation at the trailhead was marked 4,750 feet. The morning air was still cool. Sierra hitched up her wool socks and stomped her heavy hiking boots on the heels.

"Is this an old Indian tradition?" Drake teased, imitating her heel stomping. "You look like a thoroughbred ready to run a race."

Her heart did some racing of its own as she looked up and read the kind expression in his eyes. "You ready?"

"I think so. I've been looking forward to this."

I've been looking forward to this, too, Sierra thought. *And I'm excited about spending time with Drake. But is he still glad we're together?*

Shane's voice interrupted her thoughts. "Okay, everybody, listen up. The hike this morning is nice and easy. We're only going about two miles. We'll stop at a place called Lava Spring. Stay on the trail. Stick together. I'll lead, and Wes will bring up the rear. If Wes passes you, you're in trouble."

"Roger-dodger, Ranger Ricky," one of the younger guys said.

Everyone laughed, and Shane called out, "Head 'em up, moo-oove 'em out!"

Sierra waited for all the eager hikers to fall in line behind Shane. She knew it was a safe guess that Amy would be the last person before Wesley. Randy took off down the trail, and Drake waited for Sierra. The trail was too narrow to walk side by side, so Sierra went first with Drake behind her, followed by Amy and Wes.

The trail's beginning provided an easy descent. As

they hiked, the group's spirits were high and so were their voices, filling the valley and frightening any form of wildlife that might be within a mile of the trail. Sierra was frustrated. She had learned to hike silently, observing the beauty around her and listening for new sounds.

The only new sounds she heard on this trip, though, were Amy's questions for Wes.

"Is this strap supposed to rub on my shoulder like this? Do I have this buckled too tightly? Was I supposed to put the moleskin you gave me on my heels before we left, or do I put it on after I have blisters?"

Sierra wished she and Drake could walk behind Wes and take their time enjoying this gentle valley. Before them spread acres of wild lupine, covering the wilderness like a royal-blue carpet. The way was dotted with pine trees, which framed a spectacular view of Mount Adams. The late morning clouds lifted, and the great mountain jutted into the heavens in all its snowcapped glory. Sierra wished she had brought her camera to capture this sight, this feeling. A faint, familiar song began to rise within her heart. Having been born and raised in the mountains, Sierra couldn't help but feel as if she were coming home.

Glancing over her shoulder, Sierra caught the look on Wesley's face when the mountain came into clear view. He felt the same thing. She could tell.

Inside she laughed to herself. *We're like Peter and Heidi on our way to see the grandfather. All we need is a couple of goats and a girl in a wheelchair.*

As quickly as the analogy came, Sierra blew it away. The last thing they needed was a girl in a wheelchair. And the way they were hiking, this group already offered several potential candidates.

The morning hikers all made it to Lava Spring without incident. When Sierra arrived, Shane and some of the other guys were peeling off their shirts and shoes, ready to go wading.

"It's going to be cold," Randy warned them. "That water was snow this morning."

Shane was the first to plunge his foot in. He let out a whoop. "You weren't kidding!"

"You know," Wes said, speaking to Shane in a way that didn't put him on the spot, "I'm not so sure it's a good idea to pollute water like that when it's so close to its natural source."

"Are you saying my feet are a source of pollution?" Shane teased. "Okay, you guys. Wes is right. We'd better not go in. I can tell you, it's freezing."

Sierra loosened her pack's arm straps and released the waistband. Before she could take it off, someone took hold of the side frame and helped her out. It was Drake.

"Thanks," Sierra said. "You want help with yours?"

"No, I got it. Thanks anyway. That was an awesome trail, wasn't it?"

Before Sierra could agree, they heard a squeal behind them. Amy had plopped down without taking off her pack, and she was now lying like an overturned beetle, with arms and legs flailing but getting nowhere.

"Somebody help me! Wesley! I'm stuck. You guys, this isn't funny!"

Sierra smiled. For the second time that morning, she wished she had her camera.

Chapter 17

*T*HE HIKERS DECIDED TO EAT LUNCH AT LAVA Spring and then head farther down the trail before setting up camp. Sierra stretched out in the midday sun beside Drake and savored her teriyaki beef jerky. She loved the sun on her face, the salty taste of jerky, and the sound of Drake's deep voice telling her about the time he had tried to catch a bird when he was a kid.

Sierra noticed that Randy had taken off and was eating by himself down by the stream. Amy was seated next to Wes so he could examine her heels for blisters.

"That's all we get to eat?" Jana asked, sitting down next to Drake. "Don't we have sandwiches or anything?"

"Nope," Sierra said. "The food they gave you to carry this morning is all you get for the whole trip. Hopefully, we'll catch some fish tonight. The map shows a fairly wide stream up ahead."

"I thought the trail mix stuff was just for snacks. I don't even like nuts."

"You want some of my jerky?" Sierra offered.

"I don't mean to complain, but I don't really like jerky either. It's too chewy."

"You need to eat something," Wes said, walking over to their group. "And drink a lot of water. You can get dehydrated pretty quickly at this altitude."

"Isn't it beautiful?" Sierra asked Wes.

He took a long swig from his canteen and glanced around them. "This would be a great campsite for tonight. The trail ascends from here." He motioned over his shoulder. "Makes for chillier nights."

Sierra wondered if Wes was finding it hard to be a follower on this trip when in so many ways he might have been a more competent leader than Shane. If he felt that way, he didn't show it. And he was sure being nice to Amy as she followed him around.

The group hit the trail half an hour later, and Wes quietly took up the rear as Shane led them uphill and across a log bridge over a silty stream. The bugs were thick, so Sierra smeared her face, hair, hands, and legs with repellent. She put on her baseball cap and pulled down the sleeves on her flannel shirt. Even though the mosquitoes flocked to her, the repellent worked well. Only one bite appeared on the back of her left hand.

Sierra watched Drake's red backpack sway as he hiked ahead of her this time. She set aside her happy mountain-girl feelings long enough to let some of her insecurities rise again. Over the last few days, she had been overwhelmed with emotions. Her feelings had taken over everything, and she was experiencing for the first time how strong they could be.

She didn't feel good about the way Randy and Amy were ignoring them. Did it have to be that way once a couple started going together?

She thought of how her feelings for Drake were different from what she had felt about Randy. *Randy was like my training wheels,* Sierra decided. *He helped to break me into this whole world of dating. He helped me keep my balance when I was just starting off. Now I can go on my own.*

Sierra liked her analogy. As the trail led into a peaceful forest of tall silver firs, Sierra pictured what it would be like tonight around the campfire, nestled in Drake's arms. Maybe they would go for a little walk and sit together on a rock, watching for shooting stars. He would kiss her, and it would be perfect—the most romantic first kiss a girl ever had.

"Wait till you see this!" Drake said. He was standing on a small rise in the forest trail a few yards ahead of her.

She caught up with him and gazed out at the sun-kissed meadow where thousands of brightly dressed wildflowers waved in the afternoon breeze, welcoming Sierra and Drake to their corner of the world.

"Wow," Sierra agreed. "It's beautiful. I love it!"

"I thought you would," Drake said, reaching over and taking her hand in his. It felt warm and strong. Drake held her hand tightly and said, "You're really at home here, aren't you?"

Sierra nodded, her eyes still drinking in the beauty stretched out before them. If she didn't have the bulky pack on, Sierra imagined Drake would wrap his arms around her and pull her close. Even though her face was covered with sticky bug repellent, Drake would look into her eyes and tell her she was enchanting, just like the meadow, and then . . .

"Are we taking a break? Tell me we're taking a break." Amy came up behind them with Wes and prepared to take off her pack.

"We're admiring the view," Drake said, casually letting go of Sierra's hand. "The others are way ahead of us."

"Can't we rest for a minute?"

"It's better if we keep going," Wes advised, adjusting the brim of his hat and surveying the meadow. "Wow. That's incredible."

"What's incredible?" Amy asked.

"Those flowers. The meadow. That view."

Amy took a glance and then looked down at her shoes. "Yeah, it's nice. My feet say it's time for a rest."

"Come on," Sierra said. She was glad Amy was at least sort of talking to them. "Let's keep going." She wondered if Wes had noticed that she and Drake had been holding hands. *Why should it matter anyway?* she thought.

The four of them hiked silently while Sierra returned to her thoughts. This was all new to her—guys, dating, dreams, hopes, and wishes. She hoped she could talk everything through with Amy once they set up their tent. Amy would understand her feelings since she had had several boyfriends before. And Amy might have some good advice for Sierra on how to keep her friendship with Randy even though she was Drake's girlfriend.

The trail continued to ascend. When they finally met up with the rest of the group at Green Timber Camp, Sierra was tired.

But now the real work began. They had to clear the ground, set up their tents, start a fire, and catch some fish for dinner. Fortunately, the group was still in high spirits, for the most part, which helped the tent set-up go quickly.

Sierra was surprised when Amy told her she had decided to share Jana's tent with her.

"Nothing personal" is all Amy said.

Sierra couldn't help but feel it was something personal. Even though Amy said everything was fine about Drake, she had turned aloof and barely made eye contact with Sierra.

As soon as Sierra had her tent up and sleeping bag rolled out, she grabbed her biodegradable soap and her cup and headed for the stream. So what if she didn't have Amy's or even Randy's friendship? She had Drake's, and that's what she really wanted.

Following the process her dad had taught her, Sierra filled her cup with the clear, cold water and walked away from the stream, where she used the soap to wash her hands, face, and neck. Then she rinsed with the cup of water and shook her hands to let them air dry. Pulling a clean bandanna from her back pocket, she patted her face and neck. Sierra took a deep breath, feeling the cool mountain breeze sweep across her face.

"All fresh and friendly now?" a voice behind her asked.

"Drake! I didn't see you sneak up on me."

"I wasn't sneaking. You have some extra soap there?" He held up his mud-caked hands. "I feel like a slob."

Sierra held out her cup and the small bottle of liquid soap. She felt like telling Drake he didn't look like a slob to her. He fit the image of a mountain man, with his thick hair all wind-blown and a strip of sunburn across his nose. Teasing him, she said, "You look like the creature from the mud lagoon."

Drake made a zombie face and came lumbering toward her, his muddy palms poised to make contact with her clean face.

"Don't even try it," she said, laughing and standing her ground with her hands on her hips.

Drake swooped toward her and grabbed her around the waist, hoisting her over his shoulder the way Wes used to do. Sierra couldn't believe how strong he was.

"Put me down, you big, scary monster," Sierra yelled, laughing and pounding Drake's back with her fists.

"Down?" Drake asked, heading for the water.

"No, don't!" Sierra squealed.

Drake stopped right at the water's edge. "Oh, I forgot." He put her down, keeping his arms around her waist. "We don't want to pollute the water, do we?"

"That's right," Wes said from behind them.

They both turned, startled to see him standing there.

Did he see the whole thing? Sierra wondered. She felt as if she had to explain that they were only playing around. But then, this was Wes, and they hadn't done anything wrong.

Drake dropped his arms from around Sierra's waist, and she walked away from the stream and sat in the dry grass. Wes quietly went about washing up. Drake lathered up with soap and was about to plunge his hands into the stream when Wes stopped him.

"Fill the cup with water and rinse away from the stream. You never want to dirty the water you might drink."

With an understanding nod, Drake followed Wesley's instructions and watched as he demonstrated. After rinsing off, Wes pulled a bandanna from his back pocket, making good use of it as a towel before tying it around his clean neck.

"You know," Wes said, "the laws of nature tend to apply to other areas of life as well. That's certainly true here."

Drake looked at Sierra and then back at Wes. "I think I missed the point."

Wes scratched his chin. A sly grin edged up the corners of his mouth. "Most people do."

Drake gave Sierra a confused look.

"What are you babbling about, Wesley?" Sierra said, irritated. All she wanted Wes to do was leave so she and Drake could be alone.

"It's simple. Don't dirty the water. Even if you're not going to drink it later, someone else will." Wes turned to go; then added, "It's never right to spoil something pure."

Chapter 18

"**W**HAT WAS THAT SUPPOSED TO MEAN?" Drake asked, sitting down next to Sierra in the tall, wild grass.

Her heart pounded, and her eyes followed her brother as he trekked back to camp, whistling as he went. She knew exactly what Wes meant. Their dad had used the same analogy once when they were backpacking and he was trying to explain to Cody why he and Katrina should remain pure with each other even though they planned to marry. Sierra was too young at the time to understand why Dad was telling Cody not to "muddy the water you're going to drink."

But she understood everything now. She was pure and innocent and had never been kissed, and in his big-brother way, Wes was warning Drake to not be the one to change any of that.

What if I'm the one who wants to change that? What difference is one kiss going to make? Sierra thought defiantly. *I want Drake to kiss me, and I don't care what Wes says.*

"Don't pay any attention to him," Sierra told Drake.

"Is he with the Environmental Protection Agency or something?"

"Something like that," Sierra said, viewing herself as the environment and Wes as the protector. "So, how do you like backpacking?"

"Even better than I thought. You were right," Drake said. He leaned back, lacing his fingers behind his head and tilting his freshly washed face toward the sky. "It's so different out here. The sounds, the colors, even the way the sun seems so much closer. It's beautiful."

Then, turning toward Sierra, he reached over and touched one of the long curls hanging over her shoulder. "And so are you," Drake said softly. "But then, you knew that, didn't you?"

Sierra felt as if Drake's compliment had suddenly caused her insides to overflow with joy. No guy had ever said anything like that to her.

"No," she admitted shyly.

Drake smiled, twisting her curl between his thumb and forefinger. "Keep pretending you don't know how beautiful you are, Sierra. It's better that way." He let go of her hair, sat up, and stretched his arms over his head, trying to pull the kinks from his shoulders.

"Drake," Sierra asked, sitting up, "are you still glad we're going out?"

"Of course. Why?"

"I don't know. Do you think people treat us differently?"

"You mean like your brother?"

"Like everyone."

Drake shrugged. "Who cares if they do? Can you rub this shoulder? I have a knot right there," he said, pointing.

Sierra got on her knees behind Drake and started to massage his shoulder. He was right. There was a big knot.

"Try turning your head to the side," Sierra said. She had had plenty of experience pounding out her brothers' sore muscles. Drake appreciated her expertise.

"How's that?" Sierra asked, after her hands began to cramp.

"Fantastic. You're much better at that than most girls," Drake said. "You want me to rub your shoulders?"

Sierra thought it would be wonderful to feel Drake's strong hands rubbing her shoulders. But when he said the words "most girls," she suddenly felt uncomfortable. It made her feel as if she was only one of many girlfriends. Not special and unique and only Sierra.

"That's okay," she said after a pause. "I'm doing all right."

"I guess we'd better go see if we can help catch some dinner."

He stood and offered Sierra a hand up. Pulling her to himself, Drake wrapped his arms around her in a close hug.

Her emotions plummeted. Instead of feeling warm and full of dreams about Drake giving her, her first kiss, Sierra felt smothered. Caught. She slowly pulled away.

"You all right?" he asked.

"Yeah. I just feel kind of grungy. You know, all that

hiking and the bug repellent and everything."

"You smell as sweet as a flower to me."

Sierra couldn't say the same thing about Drake. His face and hands may have been washed, but the rest of him smelled a little gamy when her face had been against his chest. It wasn't how she expected it to feel at all.

Drake tilted her chin up toward him with his finger. His smile showed his tenderness. "Hey, I'm not trying to rush you or anything," he said.

"I know. You're not."

She felt nervous and painfully inexperienced. Drake obviously wasn't.

"You want to go back?" Drake asked.

"We probably should."

They walked to camp hand in hand. When the others saw them arrive, Sierra couldn't help but blush, even though she knew she had done nothing to be embarrassed about.

Drake put together his fishing gear and took off with Wes. They both asked Sierra to come, but she told them to go ahead; she would catch up later. She wanted to be alone for a little bit.

Heading away from the campsite, Sierra found a boulder with a smooth surface and perched herself on it. The rock felt warm and soothing to her troubled soul. Gathering her knees up and hugging them tightly, she began to cry.

What is wrong with me? I've been so happy the past few days, and now I'm falling apart!

For nearly an hour, Sierra sat alone, crying, thinking, and offering up tattered bits of prayers. This was so unlike her. Usually, she had everything figured out. Talking to God was as natural as breathing. Now she felt confused. Her mind swelled with doubts. Doubts about herself. About Drake. About her friendship with Amy and Randy and even about her relationship with God. Her only companion was that familiar voice in the back of her head saying, *Sierra, do you know what you're doing?*

Sierra gave in. For the first time, she admitted, "No, I don't know what I'm doing. Will you teach me, Father? Show me Your way. I need You."

She felt relieved when, a few minutes later, she heard Wesley's deep voice calling her, drawing her back to the campsite. The sun had ducked behind a grove of hemlocks, and the evening breeze turned noticeably more chilly as Sierra entered the camp. She retreated to her empty tent and put on a pair of fleece sweats over her shorts and pulled on her bulky jacket.

Three small, silver-scaled fish lay on a grill over the open fire.

"I still don't see how those three fish are going to feed all of us," Jana complained. "Unless this is a reenactment of that Bible story where Jesus multiplied the food."

"He won't have to," Amy said. "You can have my share."

She and Jana were sitting close to the fire, sharing an open sleeping bag across their shoulders.

"Didn't you two bring jackets?" Shane asked.

"Mine's too scratchy," Jana said. "And hers doesn't match."

They laughed and glanced at Sierra but didn't say anything to her.

Sierra had imagined herself sitting by Drake tonight, leaning against his broad chest. But Drake had seated himself next to Shane, and they were talking earnestly about the next portion of the trip. Sierra ended up standing to the side with Wes, moving each time the unpredictable smoke changed its course. She stood as she ate, speaking little.

As the first stars made their stunning debut in the cloud-streaked sky, Shane announced that they were going to have a Bible study around the campfire. Sierra retrieved her Bible from her tent and sat down behind Drake. He turned around and invited her to scoot closer to the fire. She gladly obliged since closer to the fire meant closer to Drake. She could feel Amy and Wes watching her from across the fire ring. All the rumbling, unsettled feelings started up again in the pit of her stomach.

I'm not doing anything wrong! she silently argued with their stares.

Shane started to talk. "I thought we would discuss relationships tonight. Our relationship with God and with others. Let's open with prayer, okay?"

Sierra leaned a little closer to Drake as everyone bowed their heads. She hoped he would take her hand the way he had when they prayed together in the car the other night.

But instead of reaching for her hand, or even acknowledging that her arm was only a breath from his, Drake shifted his position away from her. Rather than feeling Drake's sheltering arm around her shoulders, Sierra was aware of a chilly night breeze passing between them.

Chapter 19

OST OF WHAT SHANE HAD TO SAY AROUND the fire were things Sierra had heard before or thought before: Save yourself for your future mate. Hold out for a hero. Become the kind of guy worthy of a princess. Trust God to bring the right person into your life at the right time.

It was all future oriented, such as planning for marriage. What about right now? Why didn't anyone ever talk about the right way to start dating? Or how to understand changing emotions?

As if Shane had heard her thoughts, he pulled a slip of paper from his Bible and said, "This is a quote from C. S. Lewis. It helped me a lot when I was trying to decide God's will for me when my emotions were overruling my logic." By the glow of his flashlight, he read, " 'Feelings come and go, and when they come, a good use can be made of them, but they cannot be our regular spiritual diet.' "

Sierra loved C. S. Lewis and had read many of his books. She thought he was a brilliant man. Even though the quote didn't sound familiar, she knew about feelings.

She had been deluged with them the past week. Sierra could honestly say she never had known her emotions could be so powerful. She wished she had someone to explain them to her.

Shane closed by challenging them to write out what they thought God wanted for them in a relationship. "Otherwise," he said, "when it comes to dating or anything else in life, it's like taking a dart and throwing it at that tree and then going over and drawing a circle around the dart and telling yourself you hit the mark. You need to draw the circle first by understanding what God wants for you. Then you'll know if your relationships hit the mark or not."

Shane closed in prayer, and everyone retreated to their tents to warm up. But Sierra lingered by the fire, hoping Drake would stick around, too. He left with Randy and Wes, and all three said good night to Sierra, practically in unison. She sat alone for a few minutes, scanning the night sky for a familiar constellation. The clouds had increased, and only a few random stars shone through. It wasn't possible to guess which constellation they belonged to since they were out on their own. Sierra felt the same way—the lonely leftover.

She could hear Amy and Jana talking softly in Jana's tent a few yards away. Some of the guys burst out laughing in their tent. Sierra retreated to her lonely abode and crawled into her sleeping bag. A dozen thoughts and feelings circled her head, buzzing like a toy airplane on a short string.

Why did Drake pull away from me at the fire? Was it because I pulled away from him down at the creek? Or did Shane's talk make him think we needed to set better goals for our relationship? Maybe he was trying to be sensitive because I said I thought people were treating us differently.

As the rest of the camp settled down, Sierra's thoughts kept spinning. *Wes must have said something to him when they were fishing.* Sierra camped on that thought a long time and concluded, *That's probably what happened. I'd better have a talk with that overly well-meaning brother of mine.*

Fumbling for her flashlight and sticking her stocking feet into her cold boots, Sierra quietly slipped out of her tent and tiptoed to the guys' area. She remembered Drake and Randy setting up a tent close to the trail. Her flashlight revealed only one pair of boots outside a small tent. That had to be Wesley's.

"Wes," she whispered, crouching down and slowly unzipping the opening. "I have to talk to you." She slipped inside and cautiously reached for his foot at the end of his sleeping bag, giving it a playful yank and saying, "It's me, Sierra. Are you awake?"

"Harumpf," he mumbled.

"Wake up, will you? I need to talk to you."

"What's wrong?" the sleepy voice asked.

She had her flashlight pointed toward the front of the tent because she knew how much Wes hated people to shine flashlights in his face. In the muted light, she saw him prop himself up. He looked as if he had a stocking cap on his head.

"You said something to Drake, didn't you?" she whispered, hoping none of the people in the nearby tents were still awake and could hear her.

"Huh?"

"Well, just listen to me, okay? Don't cut in and try to give me any advice. Just hear me out, because I've been giving this a lot of thought."

Sierra adjusted her scrunched-up, cross-legged position at the foot of his sleeping bag, and with a deep breath, she plunged in.

"I think I've been running on emotions lately, you know? Everything I've done or said has been based on how I felt. It's like I'm being swept away by my emotions, and I don't even know what I truly feel anymore."

She ran her hands through her unruly hair and said, "For instance, when Randy and I started to hold hands, I liked it. I loved the attention."

"Sierra," he whispered.

"Let me finish, okay?" She had intended to yell at her brother for whatever it was he said to Drake. Now here she was, pouring her heart out to him. "What I'm realizing is that I loved the attention more than I loved Randy. Not that I loved Randy, or that I thought I loved him and now I don't, but I mean . . . well, you know what I mean. The attention was more important than who it was coming from. Well, when Drake came over that night, he put his arm around me, and that felt even better than with Randy, you know? My feelings kept growing, and then all I could think of was whether Drake was going to kiss me."

"Sierra," he whispered again.

"Don't worry, Mr. Don't-Pollute-the-Water. He didn't kiss me. But I really, really wanted him to. And then, after you left us at the stream, I don't know why, but everything changed. I suddenly didn't want him to kiss me."

Sierra caught a quick breath and said, "He told me I was beautiful today. Do you know what that does to a woman when a guy tells her she's beautiful? I felt like I could follow him to the ends of the earth just because he paid attention to me and made me feel wonderful. Then everything flip-flopped inside of me, and I realized I didn't want to be one of his many girlfriends. Do you know what I mean? My feelings totally changed. It's like Shane's quote from Lewis. I've had a steady diet of all my feelings and nothing else. I haven't been reading my Bible, and when I try to pray, my mind wanders. I'm full of all these feelings, but you know what, Wes? I feel so empty."

He reached his hand out of the sleeping bag and gently touched her arm. "Sierra," he whispered more urgently.

"I'm such a jumble of feelings, Wes. Last week Mom told me to show her what I'm made of, and I think I'm discovering that I'm full of mush. All feelings and no substance at all."

"That's not true," he said, sitting up. Something was funny about his voice. "Listen, I've been trying to tell you—"

Sierra reached for her flashlight and shone it in the face of the man who had been hearing her confession. Her heart stopped. Before Sierra could shriek, Randy leaned over and covered her mouth with his hand.

Chapter 20

"**S**HH," RANDY URGED, HIS HAND STILL OVER her mouth. "Don't say anything. I'm going to take my hand away, but you have to promise me you won't say a word."

Sierra nodded. Her heart was pounding in her throat.

How could he have let me say all those things? I told him everything! This is so humiliating!

"Now it's your turn to listen to me," Randy whispered. "Don't say anything. Just listen."

He sat in front of her, the flashlight now tilted toward the back of the tent.

"I think you're right about your emotions being in control, Sierra. But don't beat yourself up just because you're a sensitive, emotional person."

"Randy," she whispered.

"Shh. Let me finish. We're all learning. I have to admit I was getting pretty emotionally involved when we started to hold hands. I'm glad I got to hear what you just said because now I know it meant something different to you. I was starting to think we were more than friends. I didn't know you liked Drake so much."

"Randy," she tried again.

"I'm not done. What I want to say is, don't start using guys to build your self-esteem. It's not fair to us. I think you've already decided it's Drake you want. Fine. Just know you can't have it both ways. If you go with him, I'm out of the picture."

"Randy, you're my buddy."

"Not the way I have been. Not if you have a boyfriend. I wouldn't do that to you or Drake."

"Do what?"

"You really don't get it, do you?" Randy said.

Sierra started to feel angry. Hadn't she just poured out her soul, expressing how confused and mush-headed she felt? Why did he have to throw it back at her? Fresh tears welled up, and her lower lip began to quiver. Refusing to let Randy see her cry, Sierra took the easiest way out—she camouflaged her hurt with anger.

"Just forget everything, Randy. Forget we had this talk. You're the one who doesn't understand."

He reached over and took her arm in an effort to calm her down. "Sierra," he said.

She jerked away from him and scrambled to get through the closed tent entrance. As she gave the zipper a yank, she caught her hair in it and let out a muffled yelp.

"Wait," Randy said. He leaned forward, fumbling to help with the zipper, not knowing her hair was caught.

"Don't!" Sierra snapped. She leaned too far against the side of the tent, and the whole side began to sag. "Randy!"

she called out, just as the tent caved in on them.

The flashlight was buried in the fall, and so in utter darkness and confusion, Randy and Sierra clamored over each other trying to set things right. "My hair," Sierra cried. "Let go of my hair."

"I haven't got your hair! Get off my leg. I can't move."

"My hair's caught in the zipper. Ouch! There, I got it loose. Randy? Where did the main pole go?"

"I can't see a thing. You're blocking the light."

"I am not. You're sitting on it."

From outside, Wes's voice boomed above their squabbling. "What is going on in there?"

"Get me out of here!" Sierra pleaded.

Other voices joined Wes's. "Is that Sierra in there with Randy?"

"I thought the girls were supposed to stay out of the guys' tents."

"What's she doing with Randy? I thought she was going with Drake."

"Somebody shine a light over here," Shane said.

Within three seconds, the area around the tent lit up with half a dozen spectators' flashlights. Sierra found the zipper and opened the tent the rest of the way so she could crawl out. A dozen curious faces loomed above the searching flashlights.

"Sierra," Wes said, sounding exactly like their dad when he was mad, "what were you doing? You know the rules."

"I thought it was your tent," Sierra said, wiping back a runaway tear.

"I tried to tell her," Randy called from inside the collapsed tent.

"Why did you want to get in my tent? To steal my socks?"

"No," Sierra said, glancing at their audience and then back at Wes. "I wanted to talk to you. I thought it was your tent, and I didn't think the rule applied if I was talking to my brother."

"In the middle of the night?" Shane asked.

"It was important."

"I can vouch for that," Randy called out. "It was important."

"Randy, don't say anything," Sierra pleaded. "You guys, can we forget this ever happened? It's freezing out here."

"Okay," Shane conceded. "Everyone back to bed. Their own beds."

As the group dispersed, Sierra could only imagine what they were all thinking. Especially Randy. And Drake.

She turned, and Drake stood before her.

"Are you okay?" he asked quietly.

Sierra couldn't see his expression in the dark, but she couldn't miss his broad chest wrapped in a down jacket.

"Where were you?" For some reason she felt mad at Drake. This whole mess was his fault.

"I switched tents. There was more leg room in with Wes." He turned his flashlight toward her feet. "Come on, I'll walk you home." He accompanied her the 20 or so feet back to the girls' side and to her "front door."

"Is everything all right?" he whispered.

"I don't know."

She scooted into her tent before Drake could ask any more questions. Right now she didn't want to talk to anyone, except maybe God.

Chapter 21

AFTER A RESTLESS NIGHT, SIERRA WOKE WITH cold feet and a cold nose. She had placed the hood of her sleeping bag over her head sometime during the night and pulled the drawstring so only her nose stuck out. Fiddling to undo the thing, she noticed she could see her breath.

Reluctantly, Sierra wiggled out of her warm sleeping bag and unzipped the door of her tent. Smoothing back her mane of matted curls, she poked her head out, ready to greet the new day. The new day greeted her right back with tickles of snowflakes on her upturned face. A light, powdered-sugar dusting of snow covered the campsite. All the tents bore a fine layer of snow on their seam lines, and the tree boughs looked flocked and ready for a Christmas tree lot. The campsite had turned into a fairy world.

Wes was the only one out of his tent. He wore his bandanna around his head like a pirate and was trying to start a fire.

Sierra had slept in all her warm clothes and jacket so

the only items to put on were her baseball cap and her boots, which were extremely cold. Shuffling through the silent wonderland, she joined Wes and gave him her best smile.

"Hi," she said.

"Hi."

"Am I in trouble?"

"When are you not in trouble?" Wes teased.

Sierra fed kindling into his smoldering attempt at a fire.

"What did you want to talk to me about last night?"

Sierra looked over her shoulder to make sure no one else was up. "Guys and feelings and being all mixed up."

"You're just discovering what a basket case you are?"

Sierra playfully punched her brother in the arm.

"Do it again," he said. "That felt warm."

"I'm serious. Will you help me figure all this out?"

Wes gave her a crinkle-eyed smile. "Of course." He put his arm around her, gave her a squeeze, and kissed her on top of her baseball cap. "This is a big step for you, isn't it? Asking for help, I mean. You're usually so independent."

Sierra nodded and snuggled closer to him for warmth. "Last night while I was trying to sleep, I realized I was being too independent because I was separating God from a whole area of my life. I wasn't getting off to a very good start at dating."

"It's never too late to start over. His mercies are new every morning, you know."

Sierra looked up through the trees at the stuffed cotton

sky and tried to catch a snowflake on her tongue.

"I hope my friends feel that way, too."

Behind them, they heard a tent unzip.

"Hey, it snowed!" Shane exclaimed. "Wake up, every-body. We have to get off this mountain."

They broke camp immediately, packed up, and began the steady descent back the way they had come. The wind sliced at their faces, which made the going difficult and the group silent. It was quite a contrast to their hike the day before. The trip was supposed to last another day, with them making camp three miles up the trail at the 6,000-foot elevation. That wasn't a good idea now.

Sierra and Wes seemed to be the only two who were comfortable with the snow and perhaps the only hikers prepared for the cold. Sierra encouraged the others to keep eating as they hiked and to drink even if they didn't feel thirsty. Wes briefed them on the early signs of hypothermia and made sure everyone started out with dry clothes.

The strenuous journey back provided Sierra with a lot of time to think. In some ways, this hike symbolized her adventure into dating. She realized she had entered into the experience with a light heart, enjoying every bit of it as she went along. Retracing her steps in the wind and snow made her think of three potentially stormy conversations she needed to have and how difficult they were going to be.

Her first conversation was with Amy, and Sierra launched into it when they stopped halfway for some rest and food. They were only 1,000 feet below where they had camped, yet here there was no trace of snow, and in the shelter of the forest, the wind bullied the trees but pretty much left the hikers alone.

Sierra pulled Amy off to the side, away from the others. They sat together on their backpacks, and Sierra offered Amy half of her granola bar.

"I owe you an apology," Sierra began.

"What for?"

"For the way everything started out with Drake. I knew you were interested in him, but I didn't know how much. I don't think I was listening well enough. I think I would have handled things differently if I had understood your feelings better. I'm sorry, Amy."

"It's okay," she said. "No big deal."

"Yes, it is a big deal. You told me it was fine with you if I went out with Drake, but as soon as I did, things changed between you and me. I value your friendship, Amy. I don't ever want a guy to come between us."

"Thanks, Sierra." Amy's cheeks were red from wind-burn, and her lips looked chapped. "I have to be honest with you and say that although I was really interested in Drake a few months ago, my interest started to drop off when I saw he didn't feel the same about me. Then, when he started to pay attention to you, I felt jealous. I thought if I couldn't have him, why should you?"

Sierra rubbed the tops of her thighs to warm them. "I understand."

"It wasn't right for me to think that. I had a hard time

with it when he asked you out. Now I feel okay about it. And you're right, our relationship did get kind of weird. I shouldn't have acted like everything was fine. I just didn't know what to do. Sorry I ditched you and went in Jana's tent."

"That's okay."

"Last week was a bad week for me, with my parents fighting and everything. I don't know what's going on with them, but they seemed fine when I left Monday. Things were back to normal."

"Are things back to normal with us?" Sierra asked.

"Only if we can start to walk again," Amy said. "I'm freezing."

They helped each other up and joined the group with their arms linked.

One down, two to go.

The rest of the journey, Sierra prayed. Her thoughts were coming together more clearly than they had in awhile. She had a lot to pray about.

"What a beautiful sight!" Shane said as they entered the parking lot and saw their van and trailer, the only vehicle there. "Does anyone remember where I put the keys?"

Shane quickly deflected their looks of disbelief. "I'm only kidding, you guys. Lighten up!"

Lighten up they did. The packs were eagerly stowed in the trailer, and the tired, dirty bunch packed into the van. This time Sierra ended up sitting between Amy and Jana, and the three of them slept on each others' shoulders all the way home.

When they arrived at the church parking lot, they saw evidence that it had rained earlier, but now the summer evening sun lit up soft halos around the cherry trees lining the parking lot. Everything looked just as they had left it.

"How come I feel like a different person," Amy asked, "and nothing changed here?"

"I was just thinking the same thing," Sierra said. "A little hardship is good for a person. We need to get our world rattled every now and then." Reaching for her backpack, she added, "I think it shows us what we're made of."

"Well, I can't believe this whole backpacking thing is your idea of a good time," Amy said. "I can't wait to have a hot shower and microwave something. I definitely would not have made a good pioneer woman!"

Wes handed Amy her backpack from the trailer. Sierra thought she saw a hint of a smile on his face. The right woman for Wes would be one who knew how to start a fire with one match and looked good in a bandanna.

The other weary hikers said good-bye and drove off. Randy, Drake, and Wes helped Shane unhitch the trailer and haul it around to the church's side yard. Then Shane took off, and Wes, Sierra, Randy, Amy, and Drake were the only ones left.

"You guys want to come over?" Wes asked, looking at Sierra out of the corner of his eye. She wished he hadn't invited them. Everything felt settled with Amy, but Sierra was still processing her thoughts and wanted to have a chance to talk with Drake and Randy separately.

"I don't know," Randy said, glancing at Drake and Amy. "I'd be glad to drop you two off at the Jensens', if you want."

"All I want is a hot shower. Would you mind taking me home?" Amy asked.

"Sure," Randy said.

"I'll come over," Drake said, giving Sierra one of his warm looks.

"You want a ride?" Randy asked Drake, not looking at Sierra.

"No, I'll go with Wes and Sierra," he answered.

"Hop in," Wes said.

Sierra watched Randy drive out of the parking lot, and she felt awful. Randy was doing exactly what he said he would. He had stopped being her friend.

Chapter 22

*E*VERYONE AT THE JENSENS' WAS SURPRISED TO see Sierra, Wes, and Drake home early. Mom offered towels all around and sent them to the four corners of the house to each take a shower before they were allowed to sit down and eat.

Drake borrowed some of Wes's clothes, and Sierra put on a pair of jeans and a baggy sweatshirt. It felt so different dressing this time than it had when she had gotten ready for her first date with Drake. Now she wasn't concerned about impressing him. Had roughing it on the back-packing trip done that, or were her emotions finally calming down?

After they ate, Sierra and Drake ended up on the front porch swing. This was one of the special summer moments she had dreamed of. Now that she was actually sitting next to Drake, though, it felt different from what she had expected. Probably because she knew what she needed to say.

"Drake," Sierra plunged right in, "do you have a goal for dating like Shane was talking about?"

"Yes. My goal is to spend time with you and get to know you better. Why?"

"Because I don't have any goals yet. I feel like that example Shane gave of throwing the dart at the tree and then drawing a circle around it and saying I hit the mark. I'm just not ready to go out with you yet."

"Too late. We already went out," Drake said, stretching his arm along the back of the swing and attempting to nudge Sierra closer to him.

"I mean 'go out.' You know, be together like this. Spending time with just each other." She felt his warm hand resting on her shoulder.

"What's wrong with this?" Drake asked in a low voice.

Sierra wanted to melt into his arms and say, "Nothing. This is perfect, and so are you. Forget this nagging little voice." But she couldn't.

Instead, she pursed her lips together and did the hardest thing she had done in a long time. She slowly pulled herself away from Drake and his warm closeness.

Leaning against the cold armrest of the porch swing, she faced him and said, "I have to figure this out for myself. I need to set my own goals and draw the circle first, before I start to throw the darts. Do you know what I mean?"

Drake gave her a look that was a blend of mild shock and teasing. "Are you breaking up with me after less than a week?"

"I don't know. Is that what I'm doing? All I know is

that I can't let myself get close to you like this and act as if we're going together when I haven't even figured out what that means."

She thought about her mom's comment that it was good Sierra hadn't been kissed yet because she needed to understand what she was giving away. It was beginning to make sense.

"So, what are you saying?" Drake looked surprised.

"I'm saying I want to spend time with you and get to know you this summer, but not at the exclusion of our other friends. I need to think through my goals in dating. It's not you. You haven't done anything wrong. Everything you've done has been wonderful."

Sierra looked up, hoping to catch the tears that were beginning to gather in the corners of her eyelids. "It's me," she said. "I'm too immature, I guess."

"There's nothing immature about you, Sierra."

"Well, something about me isn't ready yet. I have to get myself balanced. Do you know what I'm trying to say?"

Drake pulled his arm off the back of the swing and folded his arms across his chest. "You're saying you just want to be friends."

"More than friends," Sierra said quickly. "Buddies. Good friends, but not boyfriend and girlfriend. I want us all to be able to do things together and not to be exclusive. You know?"

"I guess." He didn't look mad. A little hurt maybe. From what Sierra had gathered, she was the first girl Drake had asked to go with him, and he was probably startled that Sierra wanted to go in reverse after such a short time together.

"It's like the backpacking trip," Sierra explained. "I've camped a lot, but this was your first time. Now you know what to do differently next time—what to take with you and what to leave behind. I'm the one who's new at dating, and you're the experienced one. You're much more comfortable with it than I am."

"This feels like the backpacking trip," Drake said, "because we're turning around and going back so soon."

"Sort of," Sierra agreed. "Is that frustrating to you?"

"Only when I get stuck out in the cold," Drake said, nodding toward Sierra's distance from him across the seat. She knew he wanted to feel her warmth and closeness the way she felt drawn to him.

"I need to figure out this whole physical affection thing for myself before I start dating, too. I mean, do you think holding hands means the same thing to you as it does to me?"

"Probably not," Drake said.

"And have you kissed a lot of girls?" Sierra continued in her up-front manner.

"Not a lot."

"What did it mean to you?"

"I don't know. It was just a kiss." Drake laughed, a tinge of nervousness showing.

"I think it needs to mean something more than that to me before I kiss a guy. It should be more than an expression of affection. I think it should be the beginning of a commitment."

"You think too much, Sierra."

"Maybe. But that's got to be better than going totally on my feelings like I have been lately. I need to find a balance."

"Does all this mean you don't want me calling or coming by?" Drake asked.

"No, of course not! You're always welcome. And I still want to do stuff together. But in a group instead of just the two of us."

"So you want to go back to where we were before we took the walk with Brutus in the park."

"Exactly," Sierra said. "Is that okay with you?"

Drake thought a minute, then pushing out his chin, he said, "Yes, I can live with that."

"Good," Sierra said with a smile. She felt about 50 pounds lighter. Instead of wondering whether Drake was going to kiss her before he left, she was thinking about calling Tawni and telling her everything that had happened and asking if she had ever written out her dating goals.

When Drake did leave, Sierra felt as if everything between them was settled. Somehow they had managed to put their relationship in reverse, and Drake could live with it.

The last person she needed to settle things with was Randy. She considered calling him right then, but it was late, and she was exhausted. She decided to wait until the next morning.

When Sierra called, Randy's mom said he'd already left to mow the yard on 52nd Street. Pulling on a pair of shorts, tennis shoes, and a T-shirt, Sierra bounded down the stairs.

"Tell Mom I'll be back in half an hour," she yelled to Wes in the kitchen.

Chapter 23

*S*IERRA HOPPED INTO THE CAR AND HEADED FOR 52nd Street. She drove by Mama Bear's Bakery, then on impulse decided to stop and run in as a customer. Mrs. Kraus was surprised to see her.

"Yes, we all survived the trip," Sierra said. "I need to buy two rolls, one with extra frosting, and three milks."

"Glad to see that a little time in the wilderness has made you appreciate the finer things in life," Mrs. Kraus said, handing Sierra the white pastry bag.

Sierra stopped counting out her change and said, "You know what, Mrs. Kraus? A little time in the wilderness has made me appreciate a lot of things."

She flew out the door and puttered in her old car over to 52nd Street. Randy had on the headphones to his Walkman and didn't hear her when she drove up.

"Randy!" Sierra yelled over the roar of the lawn mower. "Hey, Randy!"

In that moment, Sierra realized how awful her senior year would be if Randy weren't her buddy. She couldn't stand the thought of him ignoring her as he appeared to be right now.

Boldly approaching the path of the lawnmower, Sierra held out the bakery bag. "Refreshments!" she hollered.

Randy cut the motor on the mower and looked at her. He seemed cautious. Guarded. Not sure if he was happy to see her.

"Can you take a break?" Sierra asked.

"I guess."

Sierra ran to the back of her car and pulled out an old blanket her mom kept in the trunk for emergencies. They spread it in the shade of an elm and sat down.

"What's up?" Randy asked.

Handing him his usual two milks, Sierra suddenly felt like Amy, bringing food to a guy because she wanted his attention. Maybe there was something to this technique.

"I want to go back in time," Sierra said. "Back to when we were buddies."

"What about Drake?" Randy asked.

"I told him last night I just wanted to be buddies with him, too. I want all of us to go back to being good friends."

Randy took a bite of the roll and waited for Sierra to continue.

"I've realized I need to figure out quite a few things before I start to date. This is my summer to set goals and get my thoughts together before my emotions have a chance to take over." She motioned to Randy that he had a bit of white frosting on the side of his mouth. "So, what do you think? Can we go backward?"

"No," Randy said. Then he took another bite without explaining.

Sierra took a little bite of her cinnamon roll and waited.

"We can't go backward, Sierra. Only forward."

"But I want to erase a bunch of stuff. Like the night in your tent. I want you to forget everything I said that night."

"Why?"

"Because I told you everything I was feeling."

"Sierra, you probably haven't figured this out yet, but you can trust me with your feelings. Don't be afraid of them. They're part of you. I know they're going to change. Everybody's feelings change. Don't be ashamed of that."

Randy took another bite before finishing his comforting speech. "I'm glad you spilled your guts in the tent. I understand you better now. And I meant what I said. If you want to go out with another guy, I don't want to be in the way. I'll step back. I need to figure out a lot in my life, too."

"I'm not ready for a boyfriend," Sierra said. She took a bite of her roll. "Just buddies. I need a lot of buddies."

A crooked grin pulled up the corners of Randy's mouth. "Then we're buddies," he agreed.

Sierra took a long gulp of milk and savored her last bite of cinnamon roll. Over their heads, four chattering birds darted across the wide, blue sky. A squirrel ran along the telephone line before hopping to the elm and taking shelter under the thick, green leaves. Two kids across the street shrieked as they chased each other barefoot through the front yard.

Sierra leaned back on her hands and breathed in the scent of cut grass. She noticed that the little voice in the back of her head was silent. No longer was she wondering if she was doing the right thing. Everything was beginning to feel right because it was right. In balance.

Even Randy was right. They couldn't go back, only ahead. And since each step she took with her friends seemed to be bringing them closer to the Lord and to each other, Sierra had no doubt this would be her best summer ever.

Don't Miss the Captivating Stories in the Sierra Jensen Series

Close Your Eyes (#4)

Sparks fly when Sierra runs into Paul while volunteering at a shelter. But the situation gets sticky when Paul comes over for dinner and Randy shows up at the same time! Will Sierra learn to trust God for guidance in her feelings for Randy and Paul?

Don't You Wish (#3)

Sierra is excited about visiting Christy Miller in California during Easter break. She's ready to relax and leave her troubles behind. Unfortunately, a nagging "trouble" has followed her there—her sister, Tawni! Somehow, Tawni seems to win the attention of everyone . . . even a guy. Surrounded by couples, can Sierra learn to be content alone?

In Your Dreams (#2)

Sierra's junior year is nothing like she dreamed. With no job, no friends, a sick grandmother, and a neat-freak sister, her life is becoming a nightmare! And just when things start to go her way—she even gets asked out on a date—Sierra runs into Paul. How can she get him out of her head if he keeps showing up?

Only You, Sierra (#1)

During Sierra's weeklong missions trip in Europe, her family moves to a different state. Returning home, she dreads the loneliness of going to a new high school—until she meets Paul in the airport. Will she ever see this mystery man again?

Get to Know Sierra's Friend Christy Miller!

Twelve romantic adventures are just waiting to be discovered in the smash-hit "Christy Miller Series." Each captivating story tells of Christy's struggle to stick by her convictions and trust in God's timing.

A Promise Is Forever
Off on a European trip with her friends, Christy finds it difficult to keep her mind off Todd. Will God ever bring them back together?

Sweet Dreams
Christy's dreams become reality when Todd finally opens his heart to her. But her relationship with her best friend goes downhill fast when Katie starts dating a non-Christian.

A Time to Cherish
A surprise houseboat trip! Her senior year! Lots of friends! Life couldn't be better for Christy until . . .

Seventeen Wishes
Christy is off to summer camp—as a counselor for a cabin of wild fifth-grade girls.

Starry Night
Christy is torn between going to the Rose Bowl Parade with her friends or on a surprise vacation with her family.

True Friends
Christy sets out with the ski club and discovers the group is thinking of doing something more than hitting the slopes.

A Heart Full of Hope
A dazzling dream date, a jammin' job, a cool car. And lots of freedom! Christy has it all. Or does she?

Island Dreamer
It's an incredible tropical adventure when Christy celebrates her sixteenth birthday on Maui.

Surprise Endings
Christy tries out for cheerleader, learns a classmate is out to get her, and schedules two dates for the same night.

Yours Forever
Fifteen-year-old Christy does everything in her power to win Todd's attention.

A Whisper and a Wish
Christy is convinced that dreams do come true when her family moves to California and the cutest guy in school shows an interest in her.

Summer Promise
Christy spends the summer at the beach with her wealthy aunt and uncle. Will she do something she'll later regret?

Available at your favorite Christian bookstore.